On The Wing
of a Butterfly

Craig Smith

Outskirts Press, Inc.
http://www.outskirtspress.com

Paperback ISBN: 978-1-4787-8670-2
Hardback ISBN: 978-1-4787-8675-7

Library of Congress Control Number: 2017904732

Illustrations © 2017 Outskirts Press. Illustrated by Richa Kinra
All rights reserved - used with permission.

Outskirts Press and the "OP" logo are trademarks belonging to
Outskirts Press, Inc.

PRINTED IN THE UNITED STATES OF AMERICA

CHAPTER 1

• • • • • • • • • • • •

The Solitary Voice
of the Watchman

Haydn stared in silence, awestruck. The destruction was going to be total. Some distance away from his vantage point, the very earth was being transformed by massive predators. Trees, bushes, ground cover, and brush were systematically being uprooted and carried away. Haydn's heart was heavy as he watched the wholesale annihilation.

Glistening spider webs were ripped from their moorings and scooped away with the surrounding brush. The occupants of the webs, beautiful orange garden spiders, were either crushed outright or disappeared to an unknown fate with the vegetation.

Making a continuous roar, the predators were actually scraping the ground, lowering its level. The elaborate ant colonies Haydn knew to exist in the area were helpless before the onslaught. As the vegetation disappeared, insects filled the air, flying in confused desperation, sometimes directly into harm's way and at other times landing in areas that were later devastated.

At one point Haydn saw an artistically designed wasps' nest swing wildly and fall from a tree limb with only two wasps emerging before the nest was crushed with most of its inhabitants. What troubled him most was the unseen desolation—the ruin of millions of eggs and larvae that represented the future generation for so many of his neighbors.

He especially was concerned about the decimation of the mantis population. Haydn was only a few months old, but already he knew the uncertainties of his life as a praying mantis. The egg sacs recently constructed throughout the area were beyond even hope. The future was threatened, and Haydn was terrified. He crawled to the uppermost leaves of the tree and lost himself in a moment of resignation.

From his new vantage point, however, Haydn was quickly jolted from his emotion by the enormity of the view. For the first time, he realized that the ruins below him were merely a prelude to what the future would hold for him. He could see clearly a rough path recently cut through the entire area. Without delay, Haydn flew from his tree and followed the path, noticing a series of stakes in a definite design. Haydn quickly grasped that the entire woodland paradise, his world, was threatened.

Confused and downhearted, he landed on the limb of a large oak. How could this happen? Where would he and his neighbors go? What could be done to halt the advance? The problem was monumental, but Haydn knew he must do something. What he needed was a plan. He knew he would have to enlist the help of others, so he decided to meet with other insect predators that evening, and he knew where such a meeting would be likely.

It was not too late when Haydn carefully positioned himself on the top of a rock resting in a slow-moving creek. There he waited until he was confident that the area was full of other insect hunters. Then, in a strong voice, he spoke to the unseen company.

"We need to talk. I know you're there. Arachnids? Are there any arachnids?" he asked in a commanding voice.

There was no answer. Silence filled the air along with the strong scent of pine, made more pungent by the hot August night. Haydn paused and then repeated his request.

"Our world is facing destruction, and we need a plan to survive. We need to talk!"

"Who, when you say *we*, who do you mean?" said a husky voice from the dark.

"We. You, me, and everybody else that is listening. Just a short distance away from here the battle has begun. The woods are being pulled apart, and it appears the devastation will reach here and not long from now," Haydn said evenly.

"Is there a firefly nearby? Please help us. I'm a

praying mantis, and if anyone threatens you, I'll eat him in a minute."

Almost immediately a low light appeared from above Haydn's makeshift podium. The light steadily increased until Haydn was completely bathed in the illumination.

"You—when I say *you*, I mean the mantis—are certainly a large fellow," said the husky voice.

Another firefly began beaming to reveal an enormous web suspended in gossamer elegance, and near the center of the symmetrical arrangement of the web was a spider of considerable size.

"Though I admire your ability to catch food on the wing, your interruption of my dinner hour is no way to impress me. What is the meaning of all this?" asked the large spider.

Another firefly began glowing and still another. Little by little, the area became completely illuminated and Haydn approvingly viewed the increasing audience: there were a few june bugs, several mayflies, a couple mosquitoes, a variety of beetles, crickets, and a number of aquatic bugs barely perceptible in the water.

Haydn related the events of the day and tried to make as clear as possible the imminence of the threat. The audience, continually growing in number, listened in rapt attention as Haydn made his report. The presentation was interrupted once when a small, audacious jumping spider grabbed a mosquito. Haydn

immediately confronted the little spider, causing it to jump and release its catch.

"We must have a truce to meet the mutual threat," warned Haydn.

"How can we possibly have a truce when none of us gets along?" was the garden spider's reply.

"We need to work together for a while," Haydn responded.

"Who? There are barely forty of us here. How can we—"

"All of us here and everybody else. All of the beetles, the mosquitoes, the centipedes, the wasps, the ants, the mantids, the bugs, the spiders—everybody!"

"And who, could you tell me, who can bring this diverse group together? Ants and wasps can be social but exclusively so. And most of the rest of us like our independence. I cannot even stand a husband around for any longer than a day or two. I cannot imagine…I cannot begin to imagine teaming up with an enemy or a potential dinner."

Haydn rocked back and forth in a way peculiar to mantids while looking at the beautiful but dangerous garden spider. He closely regarded her web, searching its corners until he spied her cottony egg sac tucked under a leaf nearly out of sight.

"For that!" he said, pointing one of his thorny pincers toward the sac. "That's your future, that's my future, that's our future." He gestured expansively. "We must fight for our children!"

For the first time there was response from everyone. The little sound of insect applause was gratifying, but Haydn realized the huge gulf that existed between a public display of emotion and personal commitment.

"What we need are volunteers," he said. "We need to find thousands of volunteers. The enemy is strong and intelligent. They are powerful beyond belief. We'll need to have maybe even millions of volunteers."

"And now, would you please tell me how you intend to get them? A sign-up sheet?" asked the spider, still dead center in her web.

Haydn was about to answer when a rush of air enveloped the whole company and one of the fireflies abruptly disappeared as a huge, undefined shape flew over them.

"Bat!" screamed the spider in dismay. The fireflies instantly darkened and darted for cover. There was a rustling in the grass as the assembly scrambled for safety.

Haydn gently positioned himself on the underside of a leaf. He knew from experience that any fast maneuvering would tip off the radar-equipped bat. From his new location, he watched as the same bat made repeated sweeps of the area.

In minutes the spider's web was completely ruined. Haydn could hear ominous sounds from the water as some of the flying insects flew over the creek, apparently low enough to be snatched by frogs or fish just below the surface.

Before long everything was quiet again. In time, from across the creek, the sound of one cricket began in a low tenuous singsong. The lonely sound only added to the dismal mood that had fast settled on the solitary watchman. It seemed a hopeless task that lay before him. To arouse and organize such a variety of defenders was unheard of, and to resist the type of enemy he had seen that day seemed impossible.

But then his mind turned to the alternative: a non-existent future. As short and uncertain as an insect's life is, it is life and life is sweet, he reasoned. He would formulate a plan; he would get his volunteers. He would fight!

CHAPTER 2

• • • • • • • • • • • •

The Prophet in the Pasture

During the night Haydn kept thinking about possible solutions to the catastrophe facing his world, but nothing seemed adequate. Defense against such formidable odds seemed futile, especially when he considered just how fragile his world really was. While he pondered his fate, he watched the irregular flight of several bats, heard the smooth surface of the creek disturbed repeatedly, and realized in each instance the end had come for some of his peers.

Haydn didn't sleep much, and when he awakened, he was at once tired, hungry, and grumpy. Without delay he hoisted himself onto the top of his leaf and waited without much movement, only the systematic swaying back and forth in imitation of a leaf in the wind. After a while, a fly landed near him, and in an instant, Haydn grabbed it with his two pincers and quickly began eating the struggling victim.

Haydn had scarcely begun feeding when a strident young voice interrupted his breakfast. "Hippo!"

Haydn firmly held the now dead fly but kept

motionless, ready to fly if it became necessary.

"Hippo!" the voice repeated.

Haydn turned his head on its axis and looked in the direction of the voice. Not two feet away sat the black and red velveteen jumping spider as audacious as the night before.

"It's true I'm a little large, but that's not unusual for this time of year," Haydn began in an apologetic tone.

"I didn't mean fat. I mean phony—a hippo, someone who pretends to be one thing but actually is something else…a hippo."

"The word, I believe the word you are looking for is *hypocrite*," intoned the large, husky-voiced spider, unexpectedly close above Haydn. She had encased her egg sac in heavy webbing under a leaf, pulling the sides of the leaf together to form a tunnel. She sat at the entrance, all of her eyes alternately fixed on Haydn and the audacious jumping spider.

"Whatever." said the jumping spider. "I've been starving all night. His words really moved me. I felt ashamed of myself. But now, here, I see a hypo…hypo…a phony, eating as before."

Just as he finished his little speech, a mosquito unexpectedly flew near his black and red body whereupon the jumping spider leaped up and caught it, quickly delivering a fatal bite. Contentedly, he sat sucking the life from the hapless victim.

Haydn watched, entranced as the spider breakfasted

in peace, although periodically his eyes sought out the large garden spider poised above his head. He was well aware of her ability to drop suddenly on a silken line and sink her fangs into an unwary victim. But she remained still, watching the jumping spider enjoy his repast.

When the breakfast banquet seemed concluded, Haydn slowly moved a little closer to the jumping spider and a little farther from the garden spider.

"Will you eat him now that he's dehydrated?" asked Haydn.

"Heaven's no! Gross!" came the alarmed response from the jumping spider.

"Do you—that is, the plural form of *you*—do you, either or both of you have names?" asked the throaty garden spider.

"Haydn" came the mantis's reply.

"And I'm an audacious jumping spider, so you can just call me Audi. What should we call you, fatso?"

"I choose to ignore that remark, my nervous little friend. My appellation is Agatha," said the garden spider.

"If we are to be friends, that is to say collaborators, comrades if you will, we will need to be a lit-tle more respectful in our speech."

For the next hour, the two spiders and the praying mantis discussed the situation at hand. They all agreed that they needed to pool their efforts if there were to be any hope of retaining their world. However, it soon became obvious that even collectively their limited experience did not provide the necessary key for an intelligent defense. At length the discussion came to a complete standstill.

"It's plain to see we need help," said Haydn.

"Yes, there can be no doubt. But where can we go? How can we find the right answers to our many pressing questions?" asked Agatha.

Haydn sat there carefully rubbing his pincers together and rocking gently to and fro.

Audi, turning in circles in short, jerky, little movements as if in reverie, finally stood still and responded to Agatha's questions.

"I've got an idea. We have to go down to the place without trees and see Mustabug. He's smart. If anyone would have our answers, he would."

"I am not going. I cannot go…anywhere! I have my egg sac to look after," Agatha said, sniffing.

"If you're talking about going to the meadow, I don't know that I can go either," said Haydn. "The meadow is dangerous for me, Audi. Perhaps I'd better not take a—"

"Let me get this straight. You wanna save a world, but you are afraid to find any answers? We're doomed!" moaned Audi.

"Well, where exactly in the meadow are you planning to go? I'm big and I'm awkward. If a mockingbird

12

gets a look at me, I'm a goner," Haydn said.

"Who, exactly who, are you planning to meet? Who is Mustabug?" asked Agatha, still guarding the entrance to the leaf tunnel holding her egg sac.

"He's some sort of scab or something. Family goes back a long way. He's weird but he knows a lot. We can sneak to the edge of the meadow tomorrow morning and begin our search during the day.

"Haydn, you're so green, no one will ever see you in the grass. I'm the one that's at risk, but nothing scares me; I can take care of myself," said Audi.

And with that, the plan was laid. The next day would be momentous. But for the rest of that morning and afternoon, the three enjoyed the growing sense of comradeship among them. By nightfall Haydn had finally relaxed his vigilant observation of Agatha, although he continued to be cautious of her dangerous potential. Audi periodically performed his jerky little dance punctuated by short jumps throughout the day. He wandered back and forth at Haydn's feet oblivious to the mantis's penchant for munching little spiders. By the time night fell, the three had cemented a unique and meaningful friendship.

Haydn and Audi grabbed a few mosquitoes, and Agatha spent hours reconstructing her web. In due course, they all fell asleep.

Just before dawn, Haydn stretched one of his long legs and gently nudged Audi, who jerked awake and jumped a sizeable distance away from Haydn. They both remained silent as they gazed approvingly at Agatha's web. She lay exhausted and asleep at the entrance to her nursery. They decided to let her sleep and together quietly made their way to find Mustabug.

The meadow was in fact a cow pasture that lay downstream from Agatha's web and the podium rock. Haydn allowed Audi to cling to the back of his long thorax as he flew from tree to tree in the direction of the pasture. When they finally came to the edge of the woods, Haydn felt compelled to ask how Audi intended to find the mysterious Mustabug.

"We have only to follow the directions the ants gave us. Mustabug moves quite a bit, but the ants always know. They'll tell us."

It worked as Audi had said. The two of them landed at the edge of the meadow and quickly happened upon a line of ants that seemed to stretch forever in both directions. Carefully avoiding their column, Audi listened as each passing ant added a piece of information.

Carefully following instructions, and even more carefully trying to remain in tall grass for protection, the pair soon found themselves in front of a large, stinky pile of dung! Haydn was mortified.

"If this is supposed to be fun…" he began. He paused in midsentence. Audi was doing his jerky circle dance in a frenzy, obviously delighted and unconcerned about Haydn's hesitation.

For several seconds each of them responded to the setting in their contrasting ways. It was the approach of an unusual-looking beetle that finally settled Audi down and prevented Haydn from leaving. The beetle was small and mostly black with thorny legs and a sizeable "horn" protruding from his head.

"A scarab, not a scab, you little nitwit," Haydn whispered to Audi in recognition of the beetle.

"Well, what's the difference?" asked Audi. "The important thing is his mystical power. Everyone knows that scabs, er, scarabs know everything about everything. And so they should; they're immortal, you know."

"Oh, for heaven's sake!" lamented Haydn. "Are you ever…limited. Anyway, before we leave we may as well see if by some miraculous chance this dung roller does happen to know anything that might be of help to us."

"Excuse me, we were wondering if—"

"As you can see, I'm working," snapped the scarab in a cantankerous grunt. "If you desire an audience, see me in my quarters when I'm finished here."

"Well, I'll be, can you imagine? An uppity dung roller. I can't believe it! Don't look for us. We absolutely will not—"

Before Haydn could continue his insulting remarks, Audi interrupted him by leaping on his thorax. The jump was so unexpected and sudden, Haydn stopped.

"Look at you! You're ruining everything. We need all the help we can get. Don't forget our mission. What'll

15

we tell Agatha? We need to have something to report," Audi said.

Haydn relented. Both of them followed the scarab as he rolled his dung ball toward his burrow. At the entrance were various bugs, insects, and spiders in a queue, apparently awaiting an audience with the scarab. That there was such a thirst for knowledge from Mustabug served to calm Haydn's doubts, and he and Audi took their places at the end of the line.

For a while the small group watched the scarab perform his repugnant duty, which consisted solely of forming and storing dung balls. By and by, Mustabug disappeared into the burrow for quite a while. When he reappeared, he had changed somehow. His body seemed to be glistening and he spoke with a decided accent, inviting the first of his clients to step forward and ask his question.

A male dobsonfly was quick to approach. His problem became obvious when he walked right by the scarab and ran one of his ridiculously oversized mandibles into a half-formed dung ball.

"Hey, what do you think you're doing?" yelled Mustabug. "Just leave my provisions alone!"

"Provisions? You mean I got one o' your creations on my jaw? Egad, I'm supposed to mate with these things. What am I gonna tell Cory? Tonight's my honeymoon," wailed the dobsonfly.

"Please lower your voice," intoned Mustabug. "I'm

trying to build a mood here. Just state your problem or ask your question and take off."

The dobsonfly removed his mandible from the dung and wiped it repeatedly on the grass.

"As you can tell, I'm blind," he began. "I need to know how I'm supposed to mate on the wing with these jaws when I can't even see the missus."

"That is a perplexing problem; I suggest you consult a bat. They are practically blind too, you know, and they get along just fine. There's a whole cave of them just inside the woods," said Mustabug, sounding to all the world as if he just rolled in from a foreign field.

"But if I get too close to a bat, I'll be eaten, won't I?" asked the blind and dense dobsonfly.

"Well, that is my advice," returned the scarab. "Take it or leave it. Next!"

And so it went. There was a potato bug who was worried that her appetite tended toward tomatoes; an exhausted wolf spider wanted relief from her children, who remained clustered on her body even though they were half grown; a mayfly and a june bug, who were born in June and May respectively, wanted to know why. In each case Mustabug, the scarab, gave simple, silly, or downright dangerous advice that seemed to satisfy each of the inquirers. Haydn was alternately disgusted and entertained by the series of questions and answers. He was also positive that he and Audie would be given a foolish reply. Audi, on the other hand, sat in

rapt attention the entire time, occasionally murmuring "brilliant" or "inspired" at the scarab's various responses.

Finally it was their turn, and Haydn and Audi approached together. Audi began his little dance almost immediately, forcing Haydn to carry the conversation ball.

"Our problem is also your problem—" Haydn began.

"Please," interrupted the scarab, "I don't even know you. Introductions are in order."

"Pardon me," Haydn responded, irritation in his voice. "This is Audi and I'm Haydn. As I was trying to say, just beyond this meadow an enemy is amassing, who is worse than anything we've ever experienced. Worse than bats, worse than mockingbirds, worse than anything. This great enemy tears up bushes, trees, everything. Our entire world will be destroyed!" Haydn's voice rose to the occasion.

Mustabug, the scarab, listened intently and did not respond as usual. It took a few minutes before he asked, "What does this enemy look like?"

Haydn began to describe the heavy construction equipment in the best way he could. The scarab sat in silence, transfixed, and then he disappeared into his hole. In a while, he returned smelling of fresh dung. In a voice with no accent, and with his face as set and serious as marble, he gave his advice.

"We need to organize. First, we need an area that

will allow for a proper defense. Second, we have to collect intelligence. I have much already, but the mosquitoes have the real key to the problem, I think. We must
consult the mosquitoes. Third, we need to gather an
army."

Haydn was pleasantly surprised at the incisive reply of the beetle and added his own comment. "I agree
with you. Everyone in the woods must be a part of the
defense. But how do we go about securing their cooperation? Such diverse groups as these will not readily
cooperate."

"We need to send the right messenger to each group
and patiently make them understand," said Mustabug.
"Let me see, I'll take the mosquitoes, the flies, the ants,
the hornets, and the wasps. Audi, you'll have the bees,
the aquatic ones, the field spiders, and…and…oh yes,
get the centipedes and earwigs too. Haydn, I want you
to speak to—"

"I'll work with Audi," Haydn interrupted, irritated
that Mustabug had assumed control. "Besides what you
asked him, I'll also contact the cicadas and crickets.
We'll need an early warning system."

"Agreed," said Mustabug. "We also need to contact
the Untouchables," he added in a low voice.

At this, the audacious jumping spider jerked and
whirled several times before leaping at and landing on
Mustabug's back.

"Get off me, you impudent little—"

"Stop it, both of you!" Haydn commanded. "Audi, calm down, or should I say get down off of his back and stop confusing matters."

"All right," Audi responded. "But we can't visit the Untouchables. That's suicide! Nobody that goes near them ever returns. I just will not go. Nope, I won't go. You can't make me."

Haydn sighed and offered to go himself against the torrent of advice from Audi.

During the entire exchange, Mustabug sat next to the half-finished dung ball that earlier had been pierced by the blind, and now quite possibly dead, dobsonfly. Haydn thought he was eating and tried not to look at him. But after some time, he grew annoyed with Audi's constant fidgeting and moved next to Mustabug. It was only then that he could see the scarab was not eating but rather using a dung ball to draw a fairly detailed map of their woodland, their world. The map seemed accurate, and Haydn could see that the scarab had paid close attention to his description of the current invasion.

"One thing puzzles me," Haydn said as he studied the map. "What are these Xs labeled 'known markers'?"

Mustabug slipped into his mysterious accent, remembering his role of seer and prophet. "For months I've received and coordinated reports about markers placed throughout the woods."

"Who reported them?" asked Audi.

"I have my sources. They are many and they are

accurate," the scarab said and smiled. "But enough of this. We need to begin working on our assigned tasks. At the present rate of destruction, I would estimate we have less than one cycle of the moon."

"Before we leave," Haydn said, "what are we supposed to ask our volunteers to do? There needs to be coordination."

"Just get them to spread the word among their friends. Get a representative from each group to assemble at the next full moon; that's about seven suns from now," replied Mustabug.

"Let's have everyone meet at the large rock up the creek. That's centrally located and easy to find," Haydn said.

"May the spirit of the great rhinoceros scarab be with all of us," Mustabug added.

As the scarab said his last words, he put his hind legs up on the dung ball and began pushing on the ground with his front legs, moving his precious cargo toward the burrow. In an instant he was gone, and Audi and Haydn were alone. Everything was silent except for a low rumble in the direction of the incursion. Haydn and Audi carefully edged their way out of the meadow and waited near a tree until dusk before they made their way back to Agatha's web by the creek.

When Haydn and Audi arrived back at the web they found Agatha dining on a large moth that lay inside a small web cocoon. Agatha sucked up the juices with her lethal fangs, which Haydn noticed were quite large. She didn't speak until she had finished eating and tucked her fangs against the underside of her head.

After she appeared totally relaxed, Haydn and Audi took turns explaining to the garden spider what had transpired. Haydn did the bulk of the talking, occasionally being interrupted with lavish praises for the scarab by Audi who kept twitching and jerking until Agatha thought she would scream. When Haydn got to the part about the Untouchables, Audi did scream and Agatha dropped from her web.

"The Untouchables?" she whispered. "You cannot...you simply cannot be serious!"

"Who in blazes are the Untouchables?" Haydn asked impatiently.

"It does not...it cannot be of importance to enlist their support. They do not get along with anyone, not even themselves. They are ruthless; they are without scruple or friend."

"Mustabug says they need to be alerted, and alert them we will," Haydn retorted. "Where do they live?"

"They are in the direction of the pond. Their exact location is a guarded secret," Agatha rasped in an agitated voice.

"Well, then we'll worry about them later. Tomorrow Audi and I shall visit the bees. Now that that is settled, let's eat," suggested Haydn as he perched himself on a leaf and awaited a passing meal.

CHAPTER 3

. . . .

Honey, Her Queen, and the Protocol Drone

The next day Audi was not to be found. Haydn had awakened to the sound of Agatha humming softly as she wound a silk cocoon around a moth. He was not as hungry as he was annoyed that Audi was gone when there wasn't a moment to lose. He hadn't the slightest idea how to make contact with the bees, let alone how to organize them.

"Agatha, do you know where that audacious jumping spider is?" inquired Haydn with as little irritation in his voice as he could manage.

"No, in fact I do not know where precisely he is. You cannot expect me to babysit for that little scamp. He may be, well, in fact, is a part of our large family, but that whole clan is shiftless. They never settle down, and they will not keep a normal home. It's no wonder that Audi is so nervous and jumpy. If—"

"Excuse me for interrupting," said Haydn, "but I have to find him so we can begin trying to organize the bees. Did he say where he'd be today?"

"Not exactly," said Agatha slowly. "He did say something about getting an early start."

"Oh, that's fine, just great!" snorted Haydn. "How am I supposed to carry out my assignment and worry about that impetuous little…well, I'll just have to handle the bees by myself. Good-bye, Agatha."

"Carry on without me," she said as she moved back toward the moth cocoon. "I am going to eat before I begin my day."

Haydn flew nearly to the top of a fir tree so he could get a good view of the terrain. "Where would there be a lot of bees?" he wondered. "How can contact be made? How can I recruit a few hundred thousand allies?"

From his perch he could see a small glade below with a number of brightly colored poppies growing wild by the creek. He decided that this would be his best place to begin. Before leaving the relative security of the tree, Haydn waited to see if he could observe any potential enemies. After a short time, he leaped into the air and started down toward the poppies. Suddenly, out of the corner of his eye, he caught sight of a mockingbird that had caught sight of him. There was no way for Haydn to outfly a mockingbird. His first instinct was to give up and be eaten. But then an idea came to him.

Just before the mockingbird intercepted his flight, Haydn turned sharply and quit flying; he dropped straight like a stone to the earth. The bird was confused by the swift defensive action and completely lost sight of Haydn, who landed almost exactly in the middle of the poppy patch.

The crash landing knocked the wind out of the mantis who lay in the grass under the poppies, safe but shaken. In a few minutes, when he felt secure, he lifted up on his legs and carefully walked toward one of the poppies. All at once Haydn became aware of some commotion in one of the poppies just above his head. Presently, the flower lurched to one side and Haydn was amazed to see a honeybee rolling on the grass with Audi somehow caught in her wings. The bee was buzzing curses in twelve separate dialects. Haydn couldn't make it all out, but the thought was clear enough: she wanted nothing to do with Audi.

"Audi! Let go of her at once!" ordered Haydn.

Audi was so taken by surprise at Haydn's unexpected appearance that he leaped up at an angle, landing out of sight of the mantis and the bee.

"Excuse me, miss," Haydn began.

"Say, what is this anyway? First a spider and now you. Are you dining in pairs nowadays?"

"We're not trying to eat you," he reassured her. "We want your help. You see there's a terrible enemy threatening to ruin our whole world."

"And I'm supposed to help you and a lousy little spider stop it?" The bee was now totally recovered from her tumble, and rather than appear frightened to be within reach of the mantis, she was aggravated and in no mood to listen.

"Forget it! I'm a working girl; I have a quota to make, and I won't let the hive down for some foolish little game that will no doubt end up with me being eaten by a clumsy spider and a pious-looking bug! Good-bye!" she said and off she flew.

Haydn awaited Audi's reappearance with increasing irritation. He didn't wait long. Audi, in fits and starts, came out of the grass and was just about to speak when Haydn snatched him up with his pincers and held him in midair. Audi was so startled that all of his eyes were bulging in fright. Sensing that he was overreacting, Haydn put the arachnid down and tried to collect his thoughts.

"Listen, Audi, we are on a mission here. We will be undertaking some extremely delicate business. You just can't start jumping on others, or twitching or whirling around like you've lost your mind. Just stand still when we're talking to others; restrain yourself a little bit. Do I make myself clear?"

Most of the jumping spider's eyes had tears in them. "I can't stand still and I never could. I'm an excitable spider. I'm sorry if I'm not as sophisticated as you. Maybe I oughta just go back to Agatha and let you handle this."

Haydn was overcome with regret at the penitent little spider and told him so. Audi promised to try to be more stable, and the two of them began to walk toward another part of the poppy field. As they walked, they both saw a strange fly-like insect pass over their heads in the same direction "their" bee had taken. Haydn's personality changed instantly.

"Hop on," he said to Audi as he took flight. They followed the "fly" as it approached the unsuspected bee. As the fly darted for the bee, Haydn dropped on the fly, knocking it to the ground. Audi jumped from Haydn's back and moved away from what was obviously going to be a real fight.

Rather than a normal fly, this one was quite a bit larger than any Audi had seen. It stood fairly high off the ground on prickly looking legs and glared at them with its large, black, sinister eyes. Audi noticed a particularly fierce-looking mouth. It began a menacing approach toward Haydn, who seemed to be mesmerized. The mantis suddenly lunged forward with his wings fully extended, making him look like the fearsome hunter that he was. Before the fly could move, Haydn had grabbed it with his pincers and delivered a fatal bite to the neck. Without stopping, he proceeded to consume the entire body. Audi was aghast! It was only a short time before Haydn glanced at Audi, who sat gazing at him with wonder and pride.

"You're really something," Audi said. "It was scary at first, but you sure can take care of yourself. What was that thing anyway?"

"It was a Promachus fitchii, a bee killer," a voice

answered from above them. It was the bee they had met before. "I thank you for your courageous action, and I apologize for my earlier rudeness. May I ask you to repeat what you told me before?"

Haydn was pleased to tell her all about the encroaching enemy and their plan to organize a resistance. Audi stood as still as he could, twitching only now and again, and Haydn patted him on his velveteen back several times as he spoke to the bee. At the end of his little report, he asked the bee for the support of her hive.

"This is beyond my power to arrange," she said. "I cannot help you, but if you follow me, I will see if I can arrange for an audience with our queen."

"That's great!" said Haydn, holding Audi down when he saw the spider beginning to percolate.

"Just follow me," said the bee. "When we get to the hive, find a spot outside and wait until I come back for you. If you try to enter the hive unannounced, you'll both be stung to death."

"Thank you very much," Audi said in a voice laden with emotion. "You're a honeybee, aren't you?"

"Well yes, sonny boy, I am. That's not very specific—many bees make honey—but it'll do."

"My name is Audi and this is Haydn. What's your name?"

"Why not call me Honey," she answered as she began to take off for the hive.

Audi jumped onto Haydn's thorax, and the three

31

of them departed. They flew in a direction that took Haydn and Audi outside the area either of them knew, over the Path of Great Danger and into an open field. Haydn was uneasy about birds seeing him, but his sense of mission outweighed his reluctance to travel in the daylight.

It was a while before Haydn spotted the hive. When they arrived, Honey entered the hive immediately while Haydn and Audi waited on the ground outside. Audi was amazed to see so much activity going on overhead and started to do his little dance, which Haydn, under the circumstances, did not try to prevent.

When Honey appeared at the entrance, she smiled and signaled both of them to come up. Once on the lip of the hive, Honey gave a quick bit of instruction:

"Please listen to the queen's protocol drone. I'll see you. Thank you again for the help today."

Honey flew out of sight, and Audi and Haydn awaited the approach of the protocol drone. He was quite a bit larger than Honey and absolutely meticulous in appearance and demeanor. As they followed him into the darkened hive, they could feel a cool breeze at the hive's opening. Haydn noticed several bees deliberately standing at the entrance and fanning their wings to create the air-conditioned effect. As the drone shepherded them through the intricate passages making up the hive, Audi tried to keep in control and Haydn was distinctly on edge, knowing they were completely surrounded by

worker bees that could, under the wrong circumstance, sting them both to death. The protocol drone was apparently unaffected and began a short speech defining proper decorum before the queen.

"You must keep a few things in mind: First, the queen begins all conversations. Do not speak unless she speaks to one of you. Second, do not disagree verbally with Her Majesty; she's not used to it and it's just not done. Third, under no circumstances should you try to touch her. She is the queen! She must be treated with respect. Do you have any questions?"

"No, we don't," Haydn responded, trying to find Audi with his forelegs to quiet him with a meaningful pinch. But Audi was nowhere to be felt.

Finally, they arrived at a particularly busy area of the hive, and the drone unexpectedly announced to the unseen sovereign that her guests had arrived.

"Your Majesty, the mantis and arachnid are here!"

The hive was noisy, but Haydn could hear a decided grunting sound before a voice responded.

"Welcome to our kingdom. Thank you for killing our enemy, the persistent bee killer."

Haydn immediately understood what Honey had told the queen to gain an audience with her.

"What can we do to reward you?"

Haydn, still frantically reaching for Audi, tried to respond before the spider ruined everything.

"We don't want a reward. What we want is your

cooperation," Haydn said. He explained in detail the developments that threatened the woodland, and at the end of the discussion, he felt a surge of tension. The only thing he could hear above the buzzing of the hive was the peculiar grunting he had heard previously.

"Your Majesty—" Haydn started.

"Silence! We're listening; just give us a minute," she interrupted, fairly screaming. "You came here with a problem that does not concern us. We are concerned with production here. The hive has honey to produce, and we have millions of eggs to lay. We are in no danger, and we can be of no help."

"Well, maybe you are not personally in danger now, but what about the bees that are?" inquired Haydn.

Again there was a pause in which Haydn could hear the Queen maneuvering her body with considerable effort. After a few moments, she answered.

"Young man, bees are social insects, it is true, but we all mind our own businesses. Each hive has its own queen, and believe me, our lives preclude any extracurricular activities. We have neither the time nor inclination to interfere with anyone else. So again, thank you for your selfless efforts on our behalf…"

In midsentence the queen stopped not just the sentence but all activity. The buzzing of the hive lowered.

"Selflessness," she said slowly. "That is not a new word to us, but we have never applied it to any apart from our hive. You have made a good argument, young man. We will consider your request. We will make no promises but take the matter under advisement. You may leave us now; we have much work to do. Good day."

Immediately Haydn felt the shepherding movements of the protocol drone and was whisked back through the dark and furiously active hive. Before long he found himself at the entrance and could see the sentry and air-conditioning bees actively positioned for service. For the first time since they entered, Haydn got a look at Audi and was appalled to see him totally covered with honey. Suppressing his first instinct, Haydn invited Audi to climb on his thorax, and both of them left the hive together. Haydn decided to quickly find a tree and fly back to Agatha after dark for safety's sake. It was only after they landed that Haydn addressed his furry friend.

"How in the world did you get all that honey on you? And where were you while I was talking to Her Majesty, the Queen?"

Audi was silently trying to clean the honey off each of his eight legs, and only after he was finished did he respond to Haydn's questions.

"I didn't wanna ruin things, so while you talked, I wandered around a little. How could I help it if by chance I found the food larder? I'm just grateful I did; that stuff is delicious!"

Haydn was exasperated but said nothing, thankful

that the jumping spider hadn't done anything to spoil their mission. Both of them dozed throughout the rest of the day, and when darkness came, they flew back to Agatha's web, which was in ruins. At first Haydn was apprehensive and Audi began leaping wildly while calling out to the garden spider. In a few moments, Agatha poked her head out of the makeshift leaf nursery and greeted them warmly.

"I was just getting a little nap in before remaking my web," she said. "I had a clumsy dragonfly get caught in it today, a real oaf she was too. Ripped the moorings and completely ruined my web—a disaster. However, this is incidental to the important news. I have, on my own, managed to convince the centipedes that they should aid us!

"I didn't think I would be good, that is to say, effective at soliciting help from anyone. I am not the sort to beg, you know. But I appealed to logic."

"What'd you say?" asked Audi. "Who'd you talk to?"

"Well, this morning, just after I finished my breakfast, I saw a female centipede instructing her children in walking. (You must know coordination is everything to those folks.) Anyway, when I complimented her on her family, she melted. Like every mother, her family is important to her although her children are the ugliest… God, there is nothing like a mother's loving blindness!

"I explained the situation to her, and she said she would make all the arrangements. I am, to say the least, delighted," finished Agatha with a smile.

At the end of her report, Agatha began spinning a new web as Haydn filled her in on the day's highlights. Audi interrupted several times to detail his encounter with the bee killer and other unnecessary but exciting information. He could scarcely stay still, keeping up his little circle dance and occasionally hopping up and down. Haydn didn't mind hearing about the parts that involved him and allowed Audi to go on to some length. Agatha, though feigning interest, continued working with a faraway smile on her face, obviously pleased with her own day's work. In time she was finished with the web, and Haydn was done with the story.

"Tomorrow we must visit the pond," Haydn announced. "We must make an effort to enlist the aid of the aquatic ones."

"Just be careful; the pond is a beautiful but deadly place," Agatha warned. "I shall need to take a day off tomorrow; I'm exhausted."

"But Agatha," Haydn pleaded, "you just can't take a day off. You're still a long way from getting the help of the earwigs, crickets, and cicadas."

"All in good time," Agatha said reassuringly. "I am, after all is said and done, not as young as I once was. I need to conserve my energy. I shall be of no use if I get overtired. I get grumpy and cynical. I know my limits. I cannot—"

"OK, OK," Haydn cut in. "Audi, you and I will

38

leave at dawn. And please don't leave without me. I don't want a repeat of today."

Haydn was expecting some sort of protest from his excitable friend, but when he looked at Audi, he saw that the wiry little spider was fast asleep. Haydn and Agatha smiled at each other, and Haydn patted the top of Audi's head before he flew into a tree for the night.

CHAPTER 4

. . . .

Just Plain Zula and
the Fire Ants

It was high noon before the mantis or either of the spiders awoke the next day. Audi and Haydn concealed themselves near the creek and in no time had satisfied their hunger. Agatha awoke later and found two small moths lying helplessly in her web, weary from hours of struggling to be free. She wound both of them in webbing, eating one immediately and saving the other for later. It was going to be an unfulfilling day for all three of them.

For Mustabug, the scarab, the day would be one of his most exciting, a real switch from his usual occupation. The day after his discussion with his newfound friends was spent in what was at first glance his usual way, rolling dung balls and receiving inquiring bugs, insects, spiders, and other little creatures. A casual observer would have noticed nothing unusual, but there was a subtle change. Instead of just dispensing information, the wily scarab asked each of his clients many questions before helping them.

From this method, he was able to determine quite a bit about the enemy: their strengths, their exact line of march, their speed, and their numbers (which were surprisingly small). More and more of his clients were in fact refugees fleeing the approaching enemy. Their harrowing tales of escape were at times almost unbelievable, and the enemy's power seemed without limit; none of the creatures throughout the woodland had been able to take a stand. It appeared to be a helpless, hopeless situation. Still Mustabug sensed that the key to their defeat lay with the mosquitoes; however, his first stop would be the ants, and finding ants near a scarab's work site was not difficult. Actually Mustabug had a working relationship with a colony of red ants, and they gave each other the respect of the fellow craftsmen that they were.

On the morning his friends were sleeping in, the scarab decided to visit the ant colony. It was a simple task to follow the line of ants back to the nest and quite a shock to see the size of it. Literally thousands of ants looked like they lived in the nest, and a constant stream of them trooped into the entrance while just as many came out. For the first time, Mustabug realized he had never seen any of these ants hauling seeds or any of the usual provisions that ants are seen to carry. This perplexed him greatly, but he knew he must not be distracted from the task at hand: gaining entry into the nest.

At first he boldly approached, intending to bluff his way in as if he were one of the ants. This plan failed when a soldier ant rushed up to him with menacing jaws, demanding his immediate retreat. Mustabug was amazed to see such a display and withdrew without any protest. Not one to give up easily, he soon had another plan.

Because he was used to working tunnels, he thought he would just tumble in and quickly roll down a hole. It worked fine initially; however, the tunnel came to an underground room just inside the entrance. His tumble came to a halt at the business end of another soldier ant, who grabbed him with her oversized tusks and physically carried him outside.

He was just about to give up outside the nest, when he recognized several familiar heads who also signaled their recognition of him.

"Yoo-hoo!" called out one of the workers. "Mustabug, what are you doing here?"

"Oh, it's you, Muriel. Nice to see you," he said sullenly.

"What's the matter with you?" she asked.

"I need to see whoever runs this place. It really is quite urgent that I talk to someone in charge," he said as calmly as he could.

"Look, I'll ask Zula if she'll see you. She's on the royal council. Maybe she could be of service."

Muriel went inside, and Mustabug waited what

seemed like a mighty long time. Finally she appeared at the entrance escorted by five husky soldiers whom she introduced to Mustabug.

"Ladies, this is Mustabug, who has been granted an audience with Zula," began Muriel. "Mustabug, these are five of our ablest soldiers to escort you to her chamber. I'd like you to meet Wanda, Glendean, Madge, Cookie, and Peg."

Wanting to break the awkward pause that followed and soften their bristling faces, the scarab smiled wanly and said, "Peg, what a pretty name. May I call you Peggy?"

"No, you may not," she said evenly. "There should be no reason for you to call me at all, but if you must communicate, the name is Peg."

"I see," Mustabug said weakly.

"Anyway, we don't have time for dawdling," snorted Wanda. "If a queen wants to see you, that's her business. Our business is getting you there. And before we begin, I might caution you: This is a totally female society; we have very little use for males, and we're not used to them barging in here. I suggest you refrain from any unseemly remarks…or sounds…or smells. I've had dealings with beetles before and I must say they were unhappy occasions."

"I know what you mean," interjected Glendean. "I had one of them suckers turn on me and fire. What a stink!"

Mustabug chuckled softly but was careful to avoid eye contact with the soldiers. He knew he was no match for even one of these nasty ants. Without further delay, all six of them headed in the direction of the queen.

As they walked, the scarab noticed that they were not going deeply into the nest but rather followed a tunnel just below the surface of the ground. Periodically small cracks in the ceiling allowed light to shine through, just enough for Mustabug to peer into the chambers that extended from the left and right of the tunnel. In one of these dimly lit rooms, he noticed a grisly sight: Hanging from the ceiling were several ants, apparently dead. Their abdomens were fully bloated, probably from decay. Mustabug had heard of the torture ants inflicted on each other in their numerous wars, but he was sickened by the sight nevertheless.

It wasn't long after seeing this that the party made an abrupt right into an empty room. One of the soldiers left to announce their arrival to the queen. Then Mustabug heard a commanding voice:

"OK, everybody knock off for a few. Let's take a break. Don't wander too far off; I won't be gone long, and we've still got plenty to do before sundown."

There was the sound of a heavy load dragging in the passageway outside. The noise grew louder, and the suspense was unbearable. Finally, an enormous ant pulled herself into the chamber where the soldiers and the scarab waited.

"Your Majesty," began Wanda.

"Let's just drop the formalities, shall we?" returned the anything-but-regal-looking queen. She stared intensely at the scarab, and Mustabug noticed that she looked haggard and worn.

"OK, you ladies get out. I'll handle this," commanded the queen.

"Rules is rules," retorted Wanda. "We can't all leave you here with a stranger with unknown intentions."

"All right. Cookie, you stay. The rest of you beat it!" When they were barely out of the room, she continued.

"Frustrated old biddies! All of them think they should be queen. What a laugh! They think it's really something to be a queen in an anthill. Well, I'm here to tell you it's a lot of hot, thankless work. Oh, the honeymoon was great, but look at the price I'm paying; a few hours in the air and since then I've been laying eggs for twenty-four moons, and as you can see, I'm not even half finished," she said, slapping her hindquarters in disgust.

"No siree, I'd rather be a worker. Get out to see the sun; get some fresh air. But oh, no! All I am is an egg-laying fool!"

"Well, you do get to command the others, don't you?" asked Mustabug.

"Wrong. I'm not even the only queen. There's about six of us in this nest. We make up a royal council, but the nest is run more or less automatically. So if you've

come to meet a real queen, you've come to the wrong place. I'm not Queen Zula; I'm just plain Zula."

"And I'm Mustabug, the scarab. Nice to meet you," he replied as they both touched antennae in greeting.

"I really didn't come just to meet a queen," said the scarab. "I'm on an urgent mission, and I need the help of all the ants."

"Oh my, aren't you an ambitious one," returned Zula, wearily. "Before you go any further, let's go next door and get some refreshments."

Mustabug paused a little, realizing that the torture chamber was somewhere in the area. It dawned on him that maybe his intentions were judged unworthy and they were going to hang him from the ceiling to die. Reluctantly he followed the corpulent monarch, with Cookie constantly keeping a watchful eye on him. Sure enough, as he entered the room, he could see the horrible sight and was just about to bolt when Zula interrupted his thought.

"Want something to eat?" she offered.

"Er, uh, well…if you're serving, how can I resist?" came the halting reply.

Zula reached up and touched one of the chandelier ants who instantly regurgitated something that Zula immediately consumed.

"Um," she said, "just reach up and touch their bodies and they'll give you a little nectar."

"Why, I've never seen such a thing," Mustabug said,

relieved to know the true condition of the chandelier ants.

"We're nectar ants, or did you already know that? All of the workers bring nectar to these little beauties. They eat until their gasters are filled—"

"Gasters?" Mustabug interrupted with a smirk.

"Yes, gasters!" replied Cookie, brandishing her jaws. "Do you have a problem with that?"

"Oh no, no problem," the scarab replied. "Maybe I better just state my business."

As briefly as he could, Mustabug laid the facts before Zula and asked her to enlist the rest of the council and the nest. At the end of his plea, Zula stopped him.

"Well, I can tell you this. The chances are less than slim that the council will do anything that sounds like leaving the nest. We're not designed for mobility as you can see. Besides, what can nectar ants do to help anyway?"

She had made a good point. Up until then, the only thing the scarab thought was important was numbers, millions of insects and bugs. But she was right; numbers would be useless unless they could add to the defense.

Mustabug quit speaking and was about to excuse himself when Peg abruptly burst into the room. The other soldiers were right behind her.

"Hey, what's going on?" Zula asked irritably.

"We're being invaded," Peg responded. "We've gotta get you out of here. The invaders have already breached the nest's defenses at the gate. We've no time to lose."

Mustabug watched the soldiers literally carry Zula out of the room. He followed closely behind, not wanting to be captured by any enemy. The nest was swirling with activity as they entered the passageway outside the refreshment chamber. Worker ants were streaming by them for deeper reaches of the nest while soldiers headed back to the entrance to offer whatever protection they could.

They were not long in their escape when the dung beetle could hear sounds of the battle behind them. The soldiers also sensed the danger and found a newly dug chamber in which they placed Zula. After allowing Mustabug to enter as well, all five of them stood at the entrance to the chamber.

Outside, the passageway soon became sheer chaos. Now all the ants, soldiers included, were running deeper into the nest; apparently the colony was being overrun. The scarab couldn't help wondering if his mission had been too late, if this was the invasion that they were trying to ward off. His thoughts were cut short when a heated battle began outside their chamber.

In the dimly lit passage, the enemy could finally be seen: large ants, half again as long as the nectar ants. As quickly as they approached, Peg and Madge rushed to attack them. It was difficult to see what occurred, but the struggle ended in the death of the two soldiers. Glendean, Cookie, and Wanda entered the chamber where Zula and Mustabug waited. Obviously it was to be a life-or-death defense.

The conquering enemy entered also, and the scarab watched as the last three soldiers joined the battle. Glendean grabbed one of the attacker's legs in her mandibles and gave it a vicious bite, severing the leg about halfway down. Undaunted, the aggressor managed to position her abdomen against Glendean's body, which collapsed without further struggle.

"Stingers!" the scarab murmured. "We're doomed."

He waited next to Zula, and they watched the valiant but ultimately futile defenses of Cookie and Wanda. At length they were surrounded by the stinging giants. At first the attackers looked as if they would finish the two of them off without further delay, but without warning they withdrew. Mustabug and Zula stood still until there was silence outside.

"I wonder what happened. Why did they leave, do you think?" Mustabug finally asked.

"I don't know," responded Zula. "They're fire ants. Generally they take no prisoners. Maybe they felt we posed no threat to their taking over the nest. At any rate, you'd better leave fast before they return, which they're bound to do."

"What about you? I can't just leave you here," said Mustabug.

"And exactly how far do you think I could travel in my delicate condition?" Zula asked rhetorically, gazing at her huge abdomen. "I can scarcely move, let alone escape.

"No, I think my place is here. If they leave, I'll be needed to help replenish the nest. And if they kill me… well, at least I won't have to lay eggs anymore," she sighed.

The scarab could see it would be useless to try to persuade her. She knew her own fate better than he did, so they parted and he made his way out into the passage. Once there, he tried to remember the path they had taken to enter this part of the nest. Haltingly, he proceeded in the right direction.

The passageway was empty and silent, and strewn with the bodies of soldiers. It was curious to Mustabug that not one fire ant could be found among the dead.

"They're invincible," he thought, "but at least they don't kill just for killing's sake."

Oddly he didn't see a single living ant anywhere in the tunnel. The only life he observed was in the form of chandelier ants in several of the chambers he passed. They were still engorged with nectar and probably not viewed as a threat by the invading army. In due course, Mustabug found the entrance of what appeared to be a totally deserted nest, a huge contrast to what it was just hours before. He was about to leave when he glanced up at the rim of the entryway. There was a group of the invaders with their eyes glued on him. His heart sank.

"Hello, ladies!" he finally was able to call out. "May

I have a word with you, please?"

There was no answer as he climbed up at a steady but decidedly slow pace toward the large ants, their skins glistening red in the sun. Mustabug could now plainly see their jaws and stingers. Summoning all his courage, he addressed the one he perceived to be the leader. Trying to get their attention away from him, he began telling them of his mission and why he happened to be in the quarters of the enemy at such a time, carefully trying to separate himself from the ranks of the vanquished. Rather than disarm his foes, the scarab could feel the tension mount as he described the coming chaos. Several times he noticed them open and close their jaws almost in unison; their stingers almost appeared to quiver in the sunshine.

When he had finished his story, he realized that until that moment, he had never heard them say anything to even indicate they could understand what he was saying. So he gave them his enigmatic little smile and began to walk away. The silence was absolute, and he felt very threatened. When he felt one of them touch his back, he froze.

Mustabug was at first speechless, but when the ant withdrew its leg from his back, he decided that though they might not be friendly, they didn't seem particularly menacing to him either, so he suggested that some of them follow him to his home where he could acquaint them with his coconspirators. Then they could decide if they wanted to help. Then he slowly began to walk away, and two of them followed at a respectful distance.

So it was that the scarab and his two "friends" headed back to the dung beetle's home. They walked in silence in the deepening darkness, but Mustabug felt secure with such bodyguards. As it became totally dark, he suggested that they bed down for the night so as not to become lost. The dung beetle and his two companions were soon sleeping soundly.

Just before dawn, Mustabug awoke with a start. His partners were already moving about on alert to a perceived threat. All that could be heard was a faint crunching sound. The three of them stood silently as the sound steadily increased until it occurred to the "all-knowing" scarab what was about to befall them. Seizing the opportunity to enhance his image with his escorts, Mustabug loudly addressed the unseen intruders.

"Are you looking for me? You must know that I'm not in my office right now and these are hardly business hours. If you need advice, you must await the light of day."

The ants were at first skeptical and uneasy, but when the crunching sound subsided, the scarab could practically feel their astonishment. As the sky grew lighter, the two ants and the beetle realized they were absolutely surrounded by snails. There appeared to be thousands of them covering the entire area. The one nearest Mustabug was scrutinizing him with a wary look on his face. Then his eye twinkled as he recognized the scarab.

"Mustabug!" he said with relief in his voice. "Where have you been? Everybody has been looking for you. We've been searching for you ourselves for a long time. The world is imperiled."

Mustabug didn't recognize the old snail, but his position of seer and prophet would not allow him to reveal that fact.

"Well, I'll be. I haven't seen you in I don't know how long. You look, uh, well…old. How have you been anyway? Um, these are my two friends…" He paused as he realized that he didn't have any idea what the ants' names were. Pretending nothing was amiss, he continued speaking to the ants.

"And this is an old friend of mine…"

Not wanting to leave himself open to criticism, he changed the subject.

"Are these all your family members?" He gestured at the enormous contingent.

"No," said the snail. "Well, some of them maybe. We're in a caravan now that we've had a little rain. The wetness has allowed us to continue our search for you. We want to find out how we might help in your resistance movement."

For the life of him, Mustabug could not remember this ancient-looking snail. But there he sat with his eyes mounted on the ends of his tentacles, staring at him and his unnamed fire ant companions.

"Resistance movement? How'd you hear about that, and what could you possibly do to help?"

Patiently the snail explained that the entire woodland knew about the shared threat and of the efforts to rally a defense. Mustabug was flattered to find out that he was already being credited with a major share of the leadership. As the snail talked on, other snails gathered around until the beetle and ants were completely hemmed in.

As for helping the cause, the snail said his group would organize a program for botanical defenses. Not wanting to be in a position of asking questions, the scarab put the old snail in charge and outlined the plans for a general meeting at the podium rock. It was finally decided that the scarab, the ants, and the snails would travel together to the strategy meeting. After all, there was no way of rushing the snails, and Mustabug's nerves couldn't stand another encounter like the one he'd already had.

In that the woodland was quite damp, the elderly snail assured them that the caravan could easily reach the rendezvous on schedule. (While traveling, Mustabug learned by eavesdropping that the great snail's name was Nerva. He also came to realize that the fire ants were indeed speechless, but they evidently understood him as they always acted in harmony with his requests.)

So it was that they settled back into a slow but certain journey to their destination at the creek. On the way, the dung beetle noticed thousands of insects and bugs heading in the same direction and all of them seemed full of purpose and determination. At first the scarab hated the thought of arriving last, but eventually he realized the dramatic value of a late entrance.

CHAPTER 5

• • • • • • • • • • • • •

The Lunas Have Left
Us to Destruction

When the snail caravan finally arrived at the podium rock, Mustabug could not believe his eyes. The surrounding area contained more bugs and other insects than he had ever seen at one time: katydids, earwigs, Jerusalem crickets, field crickets, dobsonflies, sowbugs, grasshoppers, beetles of all varieties, termites, centipedes, cicadas, and horse-, house-, and dragonflies. In the water, backswimmers swam and hellgrammites wriggled while mosquitoes hovered overhead. Aside from the mosquitoes, the air was choked with a dazzling array of butterflies. And there in the middle of the rock, Mustabug spotted Haydn, Agatha, and Audi watching over the gathering with approving smiles. No one at first noticed their approach.

For their part, the two spiders and the mantis were amazed to see the variety at the gathering and overwhelmed by the numbers responding to the invasion.

Agatha had crawled out of her web and stood near Haydn, who was holding Audi inconspicuously by one of his hind legs. The mantis could feel the sheer electricity coursing through the jumping spider and did his best to make him look responsible.

As the assembly continued to expand, the crickets, then the cicadas, and finally the katydids began chirping in an exuberant, if noisy, cacophony. Hearing their sound, the butterflies gathered in an enormous aerial formation, rising, wheeling, and falling. At the height of the excitement, everyone present gradually became aware of the arrival of the vast snail caravan. At the leading edge were Nerva and a couple of his cronies, upon which Mustabug and the fire ants were perched.

The scarab and ants eventually gained access to the rock, joining Haydn and the spiders. In the excitement Haydn lost his grip on Audi's leg, and the little spider began doing his dance, whirling and hopping at a frenetic pace. It was nearly dusk before the assembly quieted to hear the speakers.

When the noise abated, the butterflies landed nearby, and Haydn and Mustabug each spoke to the assembled throng. Each shared what he knew about the invasion, regarding its size and destructiveness, and each tried to inspire the spirit of unity and resistance. At the end of their summaries, the meeting was opened to questions.

A centipede began by asking, "Exactly what is the

invasion, arachnids or ants or bees or animals or…what is it?"

"We're not sure," Haydn said. "The invaders are relatively few, maybe only a dozen or so of one type and maybe two dozen of another. The first type is the most lethal. They are noisy, huge, and yellow. Their advance is sudden and massively destructive. Some of them seem to be able to level the earth; others can rip up trees and all vegetation.

"The second type is much smaller and quieter but also very capable of destroying our world. This invader seems to be able to become attached to the first type but can disassemble at will."

At this point Mustabug interrupted, "It is these latter ones that seem to me to be the key to their defeat. I believe them to be a type of animal…Help me out, mosquitoes."

"Yes, you are right, scarab. We have had dealings with these ones. They are intelligent and deadly. We have heard them speak. They call themselves…" The mosquito paused.

It had become dark, but the numerous fireflies completely illuminated the assembled multitude and had also attracted an unwanted bat. It had silently approached and was about to begin feeding when something leaped out of the water, flew to the bat, and attached itself briefly. The bat made a squeaking noise and left without further disturbing the group.

When everyone had settled back down, the mosquito continued, "They call themselves people."

A buzz arose from the group that Haydn tried vainly to stifle.

"Can they be defeated? And if so, how?" asked a nasty-looking Jerusalem cricket.

"I don't know about defeated," the mosquito said. "They can be bitten. We do that to them. We can smell them, and then we bite them. We've never seen any die as a result but maybe if we all bit them."

"What about the big invaders? Can you smell and bite them?" asked a darkling beetle, who was standing with some other stink bugs quite apart from the others.

"No!" came the instant reply. "The big invaders seem to feel nothing."

"How can we stop them then?" called out a ladybird beetle in an almost hysterical voice.

"Calm down!" advised Agatha, holding up four of her legs. "We must remain calm. Mustabug has great intelligence, a scarab wise beyond words. We need not worry."

The crowd quieted enough for Mustabug to continue.

"We don't know yet if the invasion is unbeatable. All we can do is try. We'll begin our war strategy tonight. Tomorrow we'll begin assigning battle stations. At the present rate of advance, it will be less than fourteen suns until the enemy will be where we stand tonight.

We'll form our defenses to protect what is ours. From now on, this rock will be our headquarters. Please report here in the morning to get your assignments.

"Before retiring, we need to have at least one luna moth come to the podium rock. Is there a luna moth here tonight?"

There was no answer. After further requests went unanswered, the assembly began to drift into sleep. Eventually the fireflies all went dark, and Haydn, Audi, Mustabug, Agatha, and the two fire ants were alone on the rock in the darkness.

"I'm really worried." Mustabug was first to break the silence.

"Why? Didn't ya see all the help that showed up?" Audi asked incredulously.

"I must say, I too, am at a loss. Did we not achieve our goals of uniting, of closing our ranks as it were?" Agatha added.

"You don't understand," Haydn began slowly. "The enemy we face could have killed everyone that was here tonight—in fact, just one of them could. You have no comprehension of their destructiveness."

"That's not why I'm so worried though," said the scarab. "Did you notice there are no luna moths left in the woods?"

"Yeah, how come you wanted one of those guys anyway?" asked Audi.

"There is a legend about the lovely luna. It is said

they are uniquely gifted creatures with a definite feel for danger. They can feel the future and are never caught in disasters. And now they are gone. The lunas have left us to destruction. This is not a good sign."

"Well, we cannot, we should not, put a lot of meaning in a legend. This will only destroy our resolve. Pull yourself together," Agatha told Mustabug. "There is too much at stake; a veritable civilization depends on you."

"I'll do what I can," sighed Mustabug. "Haydn, we need to lay out our plans. Why don't you others bed down for the night?"

Agatha and the two fire ants left the rock to find a suitable place to sleep. Audi had fallen asleep already, and Haydn decided to let him sleep right where he was.

"Mustabug, what really are you so worried about? You have something else that's bothering you. What is it?"

"Two things," he said. "One is the lack of meaningful support. Did you see any spiders tonight, aside from Agatha and Audi? How about stinging insects? And only two ants."

"Oh, I didn't even pay any attention," returned Haydn, "but you're right. And despite our audience with the queen bee, apparently she will be of no help."

"The thing that worries me the most," continued Mustabug, "concerns the mosquito's comment. I do know about people. They are big animals, very intelligent, and seem to have an intense hatred for all of us.

"We should order retreat in the morning and give up the woods; it's hopeless," lamented the scarab.

Haydn sat without saying a word as the dung beetle wove a depressing view of the future. As he listened, he was watching Audi's dark form rise and fall in rhythm to his respiration. It dawned on him how fond he had grown of Audi, Agatha, and even Mustabug. Things looked bleak, he thought, but friends were worth fighting for. All they really needed was guidance and confidence. The scarab was intuitive, but he was practical. Haydn had to wrench Mustabug out of his negative viewpoint before he too fell victim to it.

"Look," Haydn said, "we can't give up now. We still have a little time. Tomorrow, send the fire ants back to their nest and have them bring back their army as soon as possible. You spread the word among the hornets and wasps, just like you said you would. Audi and I will find the Untouchables, and we'll get Agatha to use her influence over the field spiders.

"Mustabug, before you leave, you must put on a bold face and give assignments to the group. Use your own intuition; the fight cannot be lost just for lack of a good omen, but it will be lost if you lose heart because of it. Everyone has faith in you, my friend; you will need to have some faith in yourself."

That night, after everyone had gone to sleep, Haydn reflected on the previous days. How quickly things had changed from the day-to-day routine to the current, constant demand for order and disciplined action. He had always been a solitary sort in the way mantids were: independent and alone but contented and self-sufficient. He enjoyed his new role though as a leading voice in the woodland's defense. He had never been a leader nor even sought to be one, but after going through the initial organizing process and recruiting the personnel, he really did feel the need for recognition. He felt resentment building up at Mustabug's growing position of preeminence—how everyone viewed him as supreme commander when, in fact, it was Haydn who was directing everyone. It was the scarab's mystique rather than his ability, Haydn thought. But unless he wanted to splinter the resistance into competitive camps, he would have to put his personal desire for adulation aside and submit to the dung beetle figurehead. He fell asleep, mentally frustrated.

Early the next morning, Mustabug was shaking him awake.

"Look! Haydn, look!" cried the scarab in a high pitch. "The butterflies are leaving us!"

Haydn looked up with sleep still in his eyes and rocked back and forth at the sight. The air was filled with the same butterflies who just the day before had graced their meeting at the rock. Only this time the multicolored clouds formed and followed the creek toward the Path of Great Danger. In less than an hour, the last of the swallowtails completely disappeared. The emptiness was almost palpable.

Audi came hopping toward Haydn and settled under the mantis's front legs. Agatha was watching from her web. Mustabug's eyes were wide and wild. He was pacing back and forth, muttering to himself. Haydn thought the beetle was going to lose complete control at any moment. Finally Haydn grabbed the scarab with his front legs and held him in midair. He was calm as he spoke, but his voice was heavy with feeling.

"Mustabug! The defense of the woodland is imperative. You are not being asked to defend it alone, but we need to have someone to symbolize the resistance. You are the one we need. Today you must assume control. Tell everyone what his or her assignment is and instill confidence in them. If you fail your commission, our world is doomed. Our only chance is in you."

Haydn almost choked on the words, but they had their effect. The scarab stopped trembling, and after being set down, he actually looked normal again.

When Haydn and Audi left the podium rock, Mustabug had regained his composure and was assigning the troops in his mysterious accent.

The only other noteworthy development that morning was the arrival of the protocol drone. His demeanor was stately and his message terse: The queen of his hive did not want to involve her hive in any sort of violence. Only in case of extreme emergency would she allow her bees to be drawn into the conflict.

When the protocol drone finished his message, he bowed his head and flew away. There was nothing to do about her decision now, Haydn thought, so he and Audi prepared to leave on their mission.

As the spider and mantis left the area, Haydn noticed that all of the snails were silent and tucked inside their shells. The constant munching that had marked them from the first was no longer heard. This made Haydn uneasy, but again there was nothing to be done so he and Audi took off for the creek.

CHAPTER 6

· · · · · · · · · · · · ·

The Awful Army in the Pond

"Climb on my thorax," Haydn invited.

This had become Audi's favorite mode of transportation; he didn't need to be asked a second time. Haydn flew down the creek in the direction of the pond. No one ever came out and said it, but it was held as a sort of legend that the Untouchables lived by a great, square hollow tree that was beside the pond. If he could get no answers there, he would at least be able to approach the aquatic ones that lived in the pond.

When they arrived at the pond, Agatha's words of warning came back to Haydn: "the pond is dangerous."

"Audi, what are we supposed to beware of here?" Haydn asked.

The jumping spider was circling as usual but in a most subdued manner. Occasionally he would stop and scan the entire area.

"Ya gotta watch out for the usual stuff: birds, bats, and things like that. And there's a buncha things in the pond that would love to swallow us in a gulp. The fogs are the worst."

"Fogs?" Haydn questioned. "We've had plenty of fogs in the woodlands. They're helpful in escaping mockingbirds and the like. What makes these fogs so dangerous?"

As they talked, Haydn and Audi began walking along the bank of the pond. Aside from a long and boring dissertation by Audi, the only other sound was of a single bee working among some nearby wildflowers. It was quite relaxing, and Haydn found himself only half listening to the audacious jumping spider. Without warning, the little spider's voice changed.

"Haydn, don't move!"

The mantis stopped, slowly turned his head, and looked behind him. A bullfrog had silently emerged from the water and sat poised to swallow him. Its black-flecked, yellow eyes lolled out at the prospective dinner. The frog remained motionless, and Audi knew it was striking a killer's pose.

Haydn abruptly fanned out his wings, making his best defensive posture. The frog, unlike the bee killer, remained unmoved and unblinking. Audi prepared for the worst, thinking he would jump at the last instant and attempt to divert the attack, but as he watched, something began happening to the frog. Its eyes turned glassy and bulged out, its front legs quivered, and its body visibly convulsed. Then its eyes appeared to glaze over and sink back into its head as the entire frog began to shrink within its skin, as if being hollowed out. In just a few moments, all that remained of the frog was the outer layer of skin, which looked like it would blow away in the breeze.

Audi and Haydn sat speechless and horrified.

Finally Haydn whispered, "Let's get out of here."

As they started to leave, all at once the most hideous pair of black eyes emerged from behind the frog. The danger had returned. Both froze in their tracks. All of Audi's eyes stared as a huge bug rose from the water. Its eyes were enormous black orbs casting a malevolent gaze. Below the eyes, where a mouth would normally appear, a fierce-looking beak glistened in the sun. Haydn was sickened to see residue from the punctured frog dripping from the tip.

"I am Phaedra," she said in a smooth, almost hypnotic tone. "I have twice saved your lives." The mantis and spider were silent. "You would not have survived the frog just now, and last night I attacked the bat for you."

Haydn was almost paralyzed with fear, imagining this grotesque bug on the wing, but he managed to reply in a thin voice, "We are grateful on both counts."

"On the contrary," she said. "I heard what is happening to our world, and I am grateful for your efforts. I want to help. My voice carries weight here in the creek and the pond. Let me be a part, please."

Haydn listened in disbelief. He liked what she said,

and he liked how she said it. Her voice, of such strange resonance, seemed so misplaced coming from the massive, sinister-looking bug. But the voice almost transformed her whole character, giving her a handsome, feminine manner. Haydn felt he could trust her.

In no time he had explained what he felt the aquatic creatures could do to help the cause. Phaedra seemed confident that she could galvanize the pond's minions. Throughout the conversation, Audi had steadily moved in his crab-like sidestep up to and then on top of Haydn. By the end of the conversation, it was all Haydn could do to keep him off of his head. The giant water bug made no indication that she noticed. Phaedra was just about to slink back into the pond when the mantis stopped her with a question.

"Do you know who the Untouchables are?"

"Yes," she said in her mellifluous voice.

"Could you tell me where to find them?"

"I advise against your going. They are deadly, even to me."

"I must enlist their aid. Please tell me how to find them," he continued. Haydn's composure was complete again.

"There is one I know of who lives under a ledge outside the hollow tree, near its top. Do you know what adamantine is?" she asked.

"No," Haydn responded.

"It's the hardest substance known. Nothing can

penetrate it, not even love."

"Why do you tell me of this?" Haydn was curious.

"The one whom you seek is called by that name, Adamantine." Her entrancing voice trailed off, and the mantis watched her huge body disappear into the pond. He was amazed that such a creature as Phaedra would even know of love. "Interesting," he thought, "and what an ally!"

When the spell of the meeting began to wane, Haydn realized that Audi had in the end succeeded in his unconscious climb and was now perched on top of his head between his eyes.

"Would you mind?" was all the mantis said.

"Oh, uh, sorry," Audi responded. "I guess I got a little nervous."

"Just relax; it's over now. Let's wait here awhile, maybe snag us a mosquito or two and rest a bit. My nerves are jangled too."

It would be late the next day that they would seek out Adamantine.

CHAPTER 7

- - - - - - - - - - - - -

Into the Den of Wolves

While Haydn and Audi were occupied at the pond, Agatha had begun her day somewhat unnerved to see Mustabug so near hysteria. She wondered how bad any enemy could possibly be to make even the scarab feel unhinged. Agatha, however, was matter-of-fact about her assignment. She had been commissioned to make contact with and recruit the field spiders en masse. So that's what she intended to do.

Her assignment was not one she would have picked. Agatha was a garden spider, a genteel spinner of beautiful and delicate webs. The field spiders were the opposite: undisciplined, rude, and cantankerous. Instead of having stable families, they were what she had found objectionable about Audi, webless and, as a result, shiftless. But Agatha was thinking of her soon-to-be-born spiderlings and their precious future. So she put aside her feelings, but not her bearing, and made her way along the woodland floor in search of some field spiders.

Her instincts led her to a part of the forest near her home that was especially debris covered. The area was in a hollow where several fallen logs lay among piles of brush and leaves. Around the trees were a number of large rocks, some of which had tunnels dug under them by small animals but which now might conceal denizens of the insect and spider world. Big as Agatha was, she knew she was at a disadvantage out of her web and might easily be prey to one of the field spiders as she persuaded it to help, so she was cautious in her manner.

She started carefully examining the ground, looking for evidence of her quarry. Her search was quickly rewarded. Near several of the rock tunnels, she found remains of various insect species: claws, legs, antennae, and other indistinguishable body parts. Though it was rather gruesome, Agatha kept her fear in check by keeping her mind on her overall purpose. She picked a tunnel most likely to contain a field spider, climbed up on a rock above the hole, and waited.

Just before sundown Agatha observed the first tentative movement from beneath the rock; first one, then two large legs seemed to probe the outside of the burrow, apparently feeling for signs of danger. After this short investigation, the spider emerged. It was huge compared to Agatha, and she was afraid to speak, especially as the wolf spider would be hungry and she would be too tempting a target. So she kept quiet and watched the spider disappear into the woods.

Agatha was about to climb down when she was horrified to see another wolf spider exit another hole. The process was repeated many times, forcing the garden spider to realize to her dismay that she had stumbled into some sort of wolf-spider breeding grounds. She became rigid with fear and cowered all night in the hollow of her rock, listening to the subdued but definite sounds of the feeding frenzy below. While in this fearful state, she decided upon a new plan for dealing with these unruly brutes.

Early the next morning, she watched the return of the wolf pack to their dens, and only after the passage of some time did she begin spinning a beautifully ornate web. Around midday she had finished the web, caught and ate a housefly, and decided to spend the afternoon napping until early evening. She had anchored her web to the upper branches of a small bush that would put her well out of reach of the wolf pack. She snoozed in security until dusk when she began watching for signs of movement.

Agatha hadn't waited long before she watched first one, then two, and then several come forth from their burrows. Summoning her courage, she began her discourse in her husky voice.

"Ladies and gentlemen," she said, her voice slower and even lower than normal. She waited until most of them had spotted her tantalizingly close yet perfectly safe location.

"Ladies and gentlemen, we, that is to say you and I collectively, have a problem. As you know, it is not our custom as web weavers to frequent the lair of our field colleagues; this is simply not done. But this mutual problem is of such gravity that we must all put our prejudices aside and work together."

As she spoke, the garden spider issued a silken line and let herself down so she dangled perilously close to the small group of gathered wolf spiders, each of which was nearly four times her size. None of them spoke, but Agatha didn't like the way they kept moving their jaws and staring at her. Climbing back up a little for safety's sake, she continued telling them what she knew of the problem. At first, each spider listened intently and kept all eight eyes glued on the speaker. Wolf spiders are not known for their long attention spans, and in short order, the crowd began to thin out. Fearing she would lose her audience entirely, Agatha figured she'd better think of something fast.

"Well, if this isn't a privilege you would care to accept, we web weavers will handle it ourselves. Together with an audacious jumping spider and the Untouchables we—"

Her plan was working.

"Untouchables? You got Untouchables? How you get Untouchables?" one of the large males asked.

"The Untouchables are pleased...in fact, delighted...to help," Agatha lied, "for the same reason everyone else is: a way of life, the future is at stake."

It couldn't have been a more dramatic moment for Agatha; all of her legs were in motion, and the spiders' attention had been rekindled with mention of the dreadful Untouchables. But the magic of the moment was short-lived, coming to a horrifying conclusion when an unidentified beetle flew into Agatha's lifeline, plunging her down and face-to-face with one of the wolf spiders.

She stifled an involuntary shudder, and gathering all of the deportment and breeding she could muster, Agatha began gently chiding the brawny but dim-witted pack.

"You cannot, you should not, think that this problem will go away," she said, raising her front legs in a sort of appeal. Walking in a sort of circle, she addressed each spider in the group. Her bold plan was working until one of the less attentive in her audience caused her to freeze with the words, "I'm hungry!"

The spell was immediately broken, and the disposition of her audience changed. It was pointless to try to run, she realized, and reconciled herself to a merciless attack. One of the larger spiders made a rapid approach, positioning itself over the top of the relatively defenseless garden spider.

"Don't touch her!" The voice was feminine. "I'll fight; I'll bite; so back off!"

"Walk with me to the tree," she whispered to Agatha. Together they slowly walked through the pack, the garden spider under the larger wolf spider. At one point Agatha looked up and noticed the powerful jaws just above her head moving in a fearsome, grinding motion. When they reached the trunk of the tree, Agatha realized that the pack had dispersed, leaving the two females quite alone.

"You're stupid, dearie, brave but stupid. We're not much on organization around here, but we're devoted parents. I just got rid of a litter. You got any family?" she asked.

"I generally do not discuss such private matters with complete strangers," began Agatha, looking sternly at the massive wolf spider. Then her countenance softened into a weak smile. "Thank you for saving my life. I have an egg sac back in my web that should begin producing hatchlings any day."

With that, Agatha climbed the tree and the two parted company as unlikely but definitely bonded friends. It wasn't until she was high in the tree that the garden spider began trembling and crying softly until she fell into a deep sleep.

CHAPTER 8

· · · · · · · · · · · · ·

I Exist Without Love

When the sun was high the next morning, Agatha lowered herself from the tree and began her walk back to the web. She had hardly traveled any distance when a sleek, black, narrow-waisted wasp landed in front of her. Before she had time to be frightened, the wasp spoke. She was fascinated by the buzzing sound built right into its voice and the manner in which the wasp repeatedly flicked its wings.

"Ze namz Zimmonz. Ze muztabug zaid you wuz near here. Zzz, zez I zhould tranzport you to ze zquare tree zitting by ze pond. Zzz, letz go."

Without further explanation Agatha was completely taken by surprise and off her feet as the wasp grabbed her with its feet and rose from the ground.

The ride to the unusual, square, hollow "tree" was exhilarating. Agatha never knew how many bugs and other insects filled the air above the woodland. It gave her a whole new perspective and also made her happy that she was part of a great lifesaving mission. It wasn't long after landing that she found herself standing next to Haydn and Audi at the base of the hollow tree. Simmons remained with them.

The four of them began an animated conversation, trying to bring all of their exploits and progress up to date. Agatha related her encounter with the wolf spiders in a raspy excitement that caused Haydn temporarily to forget his episode at the pond. Audi, who had always glamorized wolf spiders, sat in rapt attention, his six eyes glistening with appreciation.

On the other hand, when Agatha heard about the frog and the giant water bug, she, like Haydn, forgot her own near miss. It was truly remarkable that any of them had survived the previous day. After the mutual exchange between the two groups, Simmons briefly related Mustabug's successful call on the wasps and hornets. In their fast world of flying, it was no time before all the hornets, wasps, and mud daubers had agreed to rally to the cause. Even the bumblebees in the middle of the meadow agreed to provide air support as necessary. The thrill of the moment gripped each of them as they stood there.

But the worst was yet to come; approaching the Untouchables would not be easy. Standing as they were at the base of the hollow "tree", each of them began peering up the sheer sides. Haydn especially was curious about the total lack of greenery and the absolutely symmetrical shape of the "tree". It also struck him as odd that one side of the "tree" had a section that was gone, revealing its hollow nature. Mustabug had mentioned that immense animals once lived in the "tree" and people were seen there also. All of this, of course, was legend. Now the "tree" stood vacant and somehow threatening.

"Simmons, why don't you fly up near the top and see if there is any sign of life? Phaedra was specific about the location. But be careful! This is delicate and dangerous work."

"Zzz, zoundz zeriouz. Zzz, zee you," replied Simmons.

Haydn, Agatha, and Audi gazed up at the ledge near the top. It was difficult to see anything as the "tree" was completely enshrouded in heavy shade by more familiar trees that stood nearby. Haydn watched Simmons as he flew up the side almost vertically. He landed and began walking around, flicking his wings in his peculiar way. Shortly he flew a little farther to the right and repeated these same actions. Finally, when he reached the corner, he didn't land but instead began his descent to the group below.

"Zzz zuczess! Zee in ze zhadow?"

Haydn squinted at the corner of the tree ledge and could see nothing at first. Then his eye caught the glint of what appeared to be a spider web.

"I don't know what I'm looking for," he said. "All I can see is a little line. I want to say a spider web, but that's impossible. A web couldn't be seen from this distance."

"An Untouchable's web could and would be observed," Agatha said darkly.

"You mean the Untouchables are spiders?" Audi asked incredulously. His quiet and introspective mood had vanished entirely. Haydn also appeared startled.

"They are indeed!" replied Agatha sternly. "Latrodectus mactans, to be specific."

Audi was fully energized now and began circling and hopping. Haydn watched him and heaved a sigh while Agatha ignored him altogether.

"Well, we'd better get this over with," said Haydn.

"I have a word of advice, a fundamental rule in dealing with the Untouchables: Under no circumstances— you must not—touch her web; there is no escaping it. Once you are entangled, there is no hope left for you," warned Agatha.

"Can we go now?" Audi asked excitedly.

The four of them began ascending the tree. Even Simmons opted to stay with the foot expedition. All four kept staring at the corner although there was really little to see. In fact, as they drew closer, the web appeared to be abandoned.

"I don't think anybody lives there," Audi said in a ridiculously loud whisper.

"Shhh!" hissed Agatha.

"There goes any element of surprise," Haydn said, shaking his head.

Nearly to the ledge, the four came into contact with

the first of many cables forming the stringy web. Haydn touched it with one of his forelegs and felt the strength of it. The web didn't move even a little. Haydn marveled, and Agatha suppressed a shudder. Above them, in a pitch-black crevice of the tree, the light touch of the web alerted the web's single occupant. The fangs were stimulated, and in the shadows the Untouchable moved toward the entrance of the crevice. From there she riveted her eyes on the ascending party.

Upon arrival at the first lines of webbing, Agatha refused to continue any farther. Simmons, though continuing on, kept his wings at the ready, prepared to depart in an instant. Audi seemed oblivious to any danger and actually led the group. Haydn had to remind him repeatedly to stay close and avoid any sudden movement. He kept his eyes on the intense tangles of webbing above them and was particularly watchful of the black crevice that appeared so ominously threatening. At length Haydn called a halt to the climb.

"Wait a bit," he cautioned in a whisper. "Listen!"

The mud dauber and jumping spider strained to hear something but detected nothing. Haydn could hear heavy breathing of excitement from above; he could feel the tension from the unseen foe. He began rocking back and forth on his long legs.

"Adamantine!" he called out. "Adamantine, we need to speak with you."

There was no answer. Haydn called out several more

times without response. Inside the darkened recess, the shadowy figure furtively edged closer to the light, her entire body now pulsating with anticipation and her eyes still trained on her victims, particularly the mantis. Aware of the potential danger from the mud dauber, she controlled the urge for immediate attack.

By this time Haydn could make out the outline of the web's inhabitant. He could see the glint of the red hourglass on the underside of the spider; it was all he could do to remain for any length of time and complete the mission. It was too much for Audi. He also had spotted Adamantine and began moving rapidly from left to right as quickly as Haydn had ever seen him move. The little spider seemed about to lose control, and Haydn was unsure he would be of any help if Audi got into trouble.

Trying to keep the excitement to a minimum, Haydn, as calmly as he could, began describing his mission. He was partially successful in that Audi became still, but there was only silence from within the darkened crevice. It was Agatha who next spoke up. She delivered an eloquent plea on behalf of the woodlands' inhabitants with special emphasis on the well-being of the spiders. She climaxed her speech with an impassioned appeal based on their love for their children.

"If not for us, if not for yourself, surely you are just as concerned for your egg sac as I am for mine! Can you idly watch your children be destroyed?"

At this point, the breathing above them became pronounced. A voice issued from the crevice; it was breathy and ice cold:

"There's no pain in my heart

As I sneer from above,

I'm encased in a void,

I exist without love."

Agatha made a lifeline and dropped to the ground followed closely by Simmons. Haydn grabbed Audi and joined them. The mission had failed its goal. The four returned to Agatha's web by the creek.

CHAPTER 9

· · · · · · · · · · · ·

The Uncertain Defense

Haydn was disappointed by the turn of events, but he looked forward to delivering the favorable developments at the pond to Mustabug back at the podium rock. When the four of them arrived, they found the rock covered with various forms of life. Ants of all kinds formed transport lines, bringing the head-quarters' staff a steady supply of food; crickets, cicadas, and katydids delivered breaking news from the front line (now nearer than ever); and various flying insects provided fast communication from the headquarters to the far-flung contingents of the army. In the middle of the podium rock, and at the center of the bustle, sat Mustabug.

Apparently the scarab had had some of the black ants retrieve some raw material, as the dung beetle had made maps from several of his "creations." The maps accurately portrayed the developing situation. Haydn studied each one carefully while Agatha and Audi presented Mustabug with the good news about the aquatic army and wolf spiders and the disappointing news of the Untouchables.

After the update Agatha excused herself and went to her web and Audi disappeared into the hordes of insects, leaving Haydn and Mustabug to plan their strategy while Simmons listened in respectful silence.

"Is this the latest map of the current situation?" Haydn asked.

"That's it, all right," Mustabug said with sheer satisfaction. "We know exactly how far they've come and when they're due to arrive."

"When have you planned the counterattack to begin? Where will the first battle take place?" Haydn wanted to know.

"We have observed that some of the enemy precedes the main force. They cut down the large trees to allow for the main divisions that follow. The mosquitoes have verified that these few forming the vanguard are people and they are vulnerable to attack. They should arrive in only two or three more suns. When they come, we will be waiting." Mustabug smiled his enigmatic smile.

"Who will repulse them?" Haydn wondered aloud.

"We have paper wasps and hornets by air and centipedes, a variety of beetles, and other bugs firming up a ground defense. The crickets, cicadas, and katydids are going to signal the approach."

"Sounds great!" Haydn said. "What's the plan for the divisions that follow?"

"We'll deal with that when they get here" was the reply.

Haydn's heart sank as he realized that the main attack was not even being given serious attention. So little time was left, yet there was no plan to deal with the worst part of the invasion.

"Where are the fire ants?" he inquired.

"Who knows?" Mustabug shot back. "Who needs them?"

"And why are these snails just lying around?" Haydn asked, with irritation. "I thought they were forming some sort of biological defense detail."

"I haven't the slightest idea why they're sleeping. They haven't moved since you left. We've been using their sides to draw battle maps on," the scarab said.

"Doesn't anyone grasp the seriousness of the danger we're all in? When the enemy launches its full-scale attack, we'll need every available insect, bug, spider, wasp, and anyone else to help us," Haydn said, trying hard to suppress a growing feeling of alarm.

"Where's Nerva? Good night, these snails all look the same, don't they?"

Haydn began tapping on each of the nearest snail shells while calling out to old man Nerva. After several vain attempts, he heard a muffled, indignant response.

"What?" It was Nerva.

"Come out for a while; I need to talk to you," Haydn responded.

"No! Go away!"

"I said I need to talk to you." The mantis sounded angry.

The reply was too muffled for Haydn to understand. Not wanting to waste further time, Haydn seized the snail, breaking a sort of seal that bonded the shell to the ground. Nerva was livid, boiling out of his shell in an instant.

"You idiot! What? Are you trying to kill me? Look! It hasn't rained in several suns, the woods are dry, and dryness is no friend of the snail. We're temporarily out of commission. You deliver rain, we'll move; if it stays dry, we're camping out. Good-bye!"

Nerva turned his shell back over and, after some unintelligible mumbling, became quiet again. Haydn was aghast at the response. He tried again to make Mustabug see the need for further plans, but the scarab shrugged and pretended to fall asleep near a dung ball. By this time it was getting dark, but Haydn couldn't even begin thinking of sleep with so much yet to be done. He sat rocking back and forth on his long legs, contemplating well into the night before falling into a fitful sleep.

CHAPTER 10

· · · · · · · · · · · ·

The Battle Is Joined

Haydn awoke the next morning to the chirping of cicadas high in the trees—millions of them. Then he heard the sound of their counterparts on the ground as the crickets blended in. Apparently the first skirmish was taking place. He awakened Mustabug with the news. Audi shortly joined them on the rock alternately hopping and circling.

Out on the lines, the cicadas had kept a constant lookout and were the first to see the oncoming enemy. They began chirping their warning and were quickly joined by the crickets. It was easy to spot the invaders. The mosquitoes had spotted them early and swarmed around each one. Even from the trees, the cicadas could see clouds of deer- and horseflies descending for repeated attacks.

The ground near the incursion was alive with defensive forces. Earwigs waited with raised pincers, and centipedes marched to and fro to the steady cadence kept by the click beetles, while Jerusalem crickets and june bugs waited for the first sight of the enemy. The defense was ready.

Then, unexpectedly, they received support from the rear. The droning sound of thousands of wings filled the air: Paper wasps, flying in low formation, led an attack vanguard followed by hornets, mud daubers, and bumblebees. Their appearance electrified the ground forces. The air was filled with the stinging armada for quite some time. They headed in the direction provided by the sound of the cicadas and crickets.

The last of the bumblebees had not yet disappeared when an enormous swarm of wolf spiders followed—big, hairy, brown wolf spiders. They were not in defensive position but rather formed a hideous ground assault force. At their first approach, the other creatures cowered in fear of being attacked themselves, but the spiders were determined and surprisingly disciplined (although not a few of them did forget from time to time the purpose of their mission, resulting in some fatalities among the allies). Despite this, the majority seemed single-minded and nimbly stepped over their smaller counterparts.

The spiders tried to follow the slow-moving and easily observed bumblebees. In a while, the hairy brood had disappeared in the direction of the front. Emboldened by the air force and wolf spiders, the rest of the army began swarming after them. It was a diverse and spectacular army that encircled the enemy. And the enemy was absolutely caught off guard by the magnitude of the assault. Their defenses were pitiful and destined to be short-lived.

Ten of the people were following one of the lines of known markers that would eventually lead to the podium rock. As they advanced beyond the lines of defense, they ran directly into the counterattack, which began in earnest.

The paper wasps and hornets were merciless in mounting the air attack. The people responded at first by slapping at the insect soldiers and making lots of noise. When the bumblebees joined the fray, the line broke. Four people retreated, nearly covered with stinging attackers. The other six ran for the creek. When one of them stumbled and fell, the ground forces moved in. Wolf spiders quickly covered his head and hands; centipedes and earwigs wriggled up his arms and legs, biting as they went. The suffering enemy, screaming in agony, resumed his race to the creek to meet his comrades.

As the people arrived at the creek, they seemed to remove the outer parts of their skin before plunging into the water. The deserted "skin" fairly moved with contingents of the repulsing army. The invaders, hardly in the water, began scampering out, victims of hundreds of leeches—Phaedra's crew! The cicada/cricket chorus reached a din as the six people ran and stumbled back in the direction from which they came. The enemy had been defeated!

Word swiftly began circulating back from the front.

The paper wasps were first to arrive in their tight, low-flying formation. As the details of the battle were related, Audi literally danced off the podium rock. Mustabug was delirious and marched grandly marched around the perimeter of the rock, allowing the crowd to cheer him wildly.

Haydn sat rocking back and forth. He was pleased with the result of the initial success, but he also realized this was only the first wave of the attack. What was yet to come would be much worse. "How will Mustabug perform then?" he wondered. All that adulation heaped on one scarab. Would this lone dung beetle really come through when the battle was more evenly matched?

It suddenly dawned on him that he hadn't seen Agatha all day. Irritated at Mustabug's haughty attitude, he slipped over to Agatha's web. He found her in the middle of it. Right next to her was her egg sac alive with emerging spiderlings. Agatha was smiling with parental pride and graciously accepted Haydn's subdued congratulations.

Haydn again slept fitfully, awakening with the same nightmares of destruction. Several times he dreamed he heard the cicada/cricket warning and awoke completely from his slumber. When the sun had risen, he was in no mood to deal with the scarab or to control pesky little Audi. Instead he and Agatha chatted quietly all morning as they watched the last of the spiderlings hatch and leave the web.

As the afternoon began, Haydn and Agatha could hear a distant rumble that steadily increased as the day progressed. Because the cicadas and crickets remained quiet, the mantis knew that the defense line was not yet endangered. This was somehow not comforting to him. If the rumble was that loud from a distance, he reasoned, the enemy couldn't truly even be imagined—the destructiveness would be horrendous.

As dusk began to settle over the woodland, the rumble ceased and Haydn flew up to the podium rock. There Mustabug was regaling the onlookers with humorous anecdotes and silly sayings, all in his assumed foreign accent. The mantis was disgusted but was able to mask his feelings to discuss the coming battle.

"Are we ready for tomorrow?" he asked.

"We're ready for tonight, if necessary," Mustabug replied.

"May I ask the battle plan for tomorrow?"

"Same as today. Why change a good thing?" Mustabug sounded testy.

"It will not be enough, I keep telling you; it will not be enough! Why can't I get that through your thick head?" Haydn demanded.

"Shut up! You're no longer needed here. I've decided to run the war effort myself. I'm taking sole oversight of the army, and I'll run it as I have been from right here on the podium rock. I can be contacted easily, and this elevated position allows everyone to see me...uh, for direction, that is.

"If you want to cooperate with the new arrangement, take your spider friends and get out on the lines. If not, beat it!" said the scarab sarcastically.

Haydn couldn't have been hurt more if he had been bit. He looked around and observed the faces on the crowd standing close by; the scarab really did have the popular backing. Because there was no further use in arguing, Haydn flew into a nearby poplar and waited for morning.

CHAPTER 11

· · · · · · · · · · · · ·

The Defense Disintegrates

Just after dawn, the cicadas and katydids began their warning with greater fervor than ever. Their chirping was followed closely by that of the crickets. Almost instantly the rumble of the enemy could be heard and felt. Haydn suppressed the sickening dread in his stomach as the battle was about to commence. He flew back to Agatha's web, found Audi beneath it, and after the jumping spider was positioned, flew to the front to observe the outcome.

From the outset, the tide of the battle was decidedly against the defenses. The second contingent of the enemy army had linked up with the first. The huge, yellow, armor-plated assault force looked worse than when Haydn had originally observed them. They seemed impervious to attack.

Haydn and Audi watched the wasps, hornets, and bumblebees repeatedly charge without even slowing down the enemy drive. The horse- and deerfly squadrons were unsuccessful too. The advance was speedy and destructive. The invaders had the ability to simply push small trees down, tear up all the underbrush, and gouge the earth.

The flying creatures quickly ceased their attack and the ground forces fell back to the creek with the enemy in full pursuit. At the creek, the ground forces met a catastrophic defeat, and the air force totally abandoned them. Thousands of brave spiders, centipedes, earwigs, mantids, sow bugs, beetles, and miscellaneous defenders were crushed by the onslaught. The cicadas, katydids, and crickets fell back with the collapsing front. In the confusion they had ceased chirping and retreated in disarray.

Haydn and Audi flew back to the podium rock ahead of the enemy's forward lines. There sat Mustabug with his admirers congratulating each other on the successful repulse, so they thought, signaled by the silence of the cicada/cricket warning system.

Haydn's landing on the rock provoked Mustabug to rage, "Now listen, you! I told you, we don't want you around. The battle is already over, and I'll thank you to move on."

The looks on Haydn's and Audi's faces held the scarab's lecture in check.

"What's the matter? Why do you look so glum?" inquired the dung beetle.

Haydn never had a chance to answer. Within moments, they saw the air defenses raggedly flying in full retreat, their numbers greatly depleted. Shortly, the hordes of ground forces appeared—many of them mutilated—streaming away from the battle. The air, ground, and creek were filled with an entire army battered and beaten. At first Mustabug sat staring in disbelief. Then he started to whine and finally sob, deep heaving sobs of despair and failure. He shook from head to feet, wailing and weeping in dejection. At the sight of the scarab's breakdown, all further resistance crumbled and the headquarters' staff broke into full-fledged flight with the army. Haydn's worst fears were being realized.

As calmly as he could, Haydn asked the back-flowing stream of ants to take Mustabug with them and care for him as much as possible. Then he began sending messages by some of Simmons's wasp friends to all of the army's components to regroup in the thicket around the pond. Next he instructed Simmons to take Agatha and as many of her spiderlings as they could gather and meet him at the new headquarters in the hollow tree by the pond. Haydn then grabbed Audi and left the podium rock, heading first for the pond and then to assume command at the new headquarters.

With the roar of enemy destruction close behind them, Haydn realized it finally had begun raining. He viewed with pity Nerva and the hundreds of snails that had meant to do so much and now lay helplessly in the path of the incursion. The rain had come too late.

Following the creek, Haydn observed that the water

was swelled with little creatures falling back in panic. Even the giant water bugs, their eyes bulging from their heads, seemed to have lost all resolve to fight.

When Haydn and Audi landed at the pond, the rain was falling heavily, which only seemed to make the disaster worse than ever. Haydn was deeply depressed but relieved to hear the far-off rumble of the enemy die off completely in the distance. He needed time, and maybe the rain would give him just enough. In the meantime, he needed to think. He would have to develop not merely a defensive posture but also an offensive plan in order to win the war and save the world.

He spoke quietly with Audi, who was surprisingly calm and subdued. In fact Haydn was amazed at how much control the little spider was maintaining; moreover, Audi was comforting Haydn, several times reaching up and patting the base of the mantis's long legs as he rocked back and forth. Though Audi offered no actual advice, the consolation he gave silently was what Haydn needed. They both slept soundly until the first light of day.

CHAPTER 12

• • • • • • • • • • •

Turning the Tide

Haydn awoke with a start. Standing next to him and the still-sleeping Audi was Phaedra and another giant water bug, both of them completely out of the water. She was massive and fierce looking, her eyes and beak creating a distinct, life-threatening feeling in the mantis. Her partner was nearly her exact double except for one major difference: its back was covered with a series of irregular projections that made Haydn curious and repelled at the same time.

"Have we lost everything?" Phaedra asked in a firm voice.

"No," Haydn said, "the enemy is not invulnerable; we were not properly prepared. I know how to defeat them, but I need a little time to regroup the forces. They're supposed to converge around here tomorrow sometime.

"Eh, who is—?" Curiosity had overcome the mantis.

"Oh, how rude of me. What was I thinking? This is my mate."

Looking at the odd projections on the bug's back, the

now fully awake jumping spider audaciously intruded on the conversation. "Are you sick or something?"

"No, I'm not sick, little guy. My back is covered with eggs. It may seem unusual to you, but this is how our eggs are cared for until our children are hatched."

"Oh," returned Audi.

As if she hadn't heard the exchange, Phaedra said, "Your warnings about the enemy were understated. I thought maybe you had exaggerated a little, but you were accurate. We still want to help. Incidentally, did you ever secure help from the Untouchables?"

"No, in fact, we didn't," Haydn replied.

"I didn't think you would; they are a cold-hearted lot. But we'll be successful without them."

With that, the giant water bugs walked back to the pond and disappeared into the murky water. The rest of the day passed without incident.

The next morning, Haydn and Audi flew up to the hollow tree, which was swarming with fragments of the defeated army and refugees from the woodland. The rain had stopped, but apparently the enemy was not in position to press their advantage. Haydn was optimistic as he and Audi appeared on a small ledge inside the tree above the throngs below.

"Thank you all for coming," Haydn began. "We'll need to reorganize ourselves."

"Not on your life!" a dobsonfly screamed.

"You and the audacious jumping spider have done

enough damage already," added an earwig with one of his pincers missing.

"Down with the mantis!" called out a millipede.

"Kill them both! Kill them both!" cheered the crowd.

Haydn grabbed Audi and was about to fly when they were quickly surrounded by bumblebees and mud daubers. The din of the crowd increased as the stinging insects pushed Haydn and Audi closer to the edge. Suddenly the mantis became aware of a change in the sound of the mob below. It started near the back toward the opening of the tree and rapidly worked its way through the group to the front. In fact, as the disturbance progressed, Haydn could see the multitude give way to make a path for whatever it was that approached.

He was at once shocked and relieved to see an enormous column of fire ants march toward the ledge. He noticed that some of the ants were carrying smaller ants with grotesquely misshapen abdomens. One of them, which was quite a bit larger than the others, was being both carried and pulled (some of her legs had actually been reduced in size by the pace, too rapid for her bulky body). She was brought to the area just below the ledge where her bearers unceremoniously dropped her in an undignified heap. All eyes and ears were on her.

"Where is Mustabug?" she demanded. "Where is the scarab?"

At this point a number of fire ants had made their way up to the ledge and surrounded the bumblebees and mud daubers, who at once flew out of harm's way.

"Mustabug has...he is sick," Haydn said. "He did a fine job, but his health gave out on him."

"Just as well," the ant returned. "Whoever was responsible for yesterday's defeat was to be stung to death, according to the order of the queen of these fire ants. Are you running the operation now? Have you taken over?"

"He's the best qualified," Audi responded, his little eyes sparkling down at the ant. "He tried to tell the scarab what to expect. If only Mustabug had believed him, the slaughter wouldn't have happened."

Haydn was moved by this testimonial from his furry friend.

"I know how to defeat the enemy, but I need full and complete cooperation from everyone. Can I expect that?" Haydn asked as he looked over the crowd.

"I shall relay your message to the ruler of the fire ants. I am merely acting as their spokesperson. My name is Zula and the fire ants do respect my opinions. I think they'll cooperate; they are concerned."

The audience remained silent and seemed unable to resist the developing situation or the forces of the fire ants that nearly overwhelmed the entire crowd.

For the next two days, the rain fell sporadically, slowing the enemy advance and allowing the defenses to regroup and restructure. Hordes of additional troops arrived from beyond the woodland, determined to help the embattled defenders. Haydn arranged for the paper wasps to meet with him in conjunction with the fire ants. It was an eventful meeting that began in an atmosphere of tension. The ants arrived late, and the paper wasps were even more agitated than usual. When the ants did arrive, it was obvious that they were also of an irritable nature. Several of the soldiers were carrying the ants with the misshapen abdomens.

Naturally Audi noticed the unique ant and its swollen hindquarters, immediately blurting out, "Wow! What's the matter with your friend?"

"Nothing is wrong with my friend," replied Zula, who seemed always to be with the fire ants. "Haven't you ever seen a nectar ant before? They supply nourishment. When I touch her head, she releases nectar from her gasters—"

"Gasters?" Audi interrupted and grinned.

Haydn shot him a significant glare and, reaching out, moved the jumping spider to a less conspicuous location.

"What is the meaning of this meeting?" Zula asked.

"You ants need to work in tandem with the wasps," Haydn said.

"Nothing doing. Ants work alone!" Zula responded.

"Zzzz, zame for uz," said the paper wasps. (Haydn noticed the same peculiar buzzing in the paper wasps' voices that he had noticed in Simmons'.)

"Tell us," Haydn invited, "how successful was the

attack by the wasps and hornets on the enemy in our last battle?"

"Zzzzz, unzuccezzful."

"Right. And do you know why?"

"Zzzzz, it za myztery."

"No, it's not," Haydn retorted. "The people are the vulnerable part of their army. We need to get to them. The wasps cannot do that because the people are enclosed in movable nests of some sort. The mosquitoes have penetrated the nests.

"Here's where you ants come in. The mosquitoes will locate the vulnerable people by smell and surround them. Then the wasps will drop the fire ants from the air, and when you guys land, search out the people and start stinging for all you're worth."

"Zzzzz, zoundz exziting!" replied the paper wasp.

"Oh, brother" was all Zula could say, but she agreed to give it a try. They left in peace.

To the ground and water forces, Haydn's directions were specific and conservative of life. "Wait until you see the people exit their moving nests," he told them, "and then move in and bite or sting or pinch."

"But what if they stomp us again?" objected a wolf spider.

"Yeah, where are the Untouchables anyway? That fat garden spider said they wuz gonna help out."

"Well, perhaps they just haven't arrived yet," said Haydn. "Just do your work well and don't worry about the Untouchables."

That seemed to work, and the ground forces were sent to form a line well in front of the thicket surrounding the pond and the hollow tree.

Haydn's instructions to the cicadas, katydids, and crickets were a bit more detailed. He trained them patiently to chirp in a point-counterpoint cadence so each group could hear the other in unison.

"Under no circumstances are you to stop chirping, no matter how the battle appears to be going. You are our anthem, our rallying point; we depend on your reliability."

Of course, the cicadas and their comrades were delighted to have such a major privilege accorded to them and left for their posts.

Haydn, upon completing his primary battle strategy, told Audi to look after Agatha, who had constructed a small web in the hollow tree. He told the jumping spider to answer any questions that arose the best he could because the mantis would be going on a mission. Audi was to assume temporary command until Haydn returned for the upcoming resumption of hostilities. After these instructions, Haydn flew out of the tree and disappeared.

One sun came and went, then two. Daily the parade of inquiring insects lined up on the ledge to consult with Audi, who generally deferred their questions until Haydn's return. Each passing sun seemed endless to Audi and Agatha. They began to suspect that something dreadful had happened to Haydn and at the worst possible time.

On the fourth sun, with the enemy closing in, the headquarters was disturbed early in the morning by a familiar and welcome sound: munching. Somehow Nerva and the snails had survived the advance. They explained that the rain had halted the enemy in time to allow them to break camp. Following the lines of transport ants had led them to the new headquarters. They also reported that the podium rock had been mashed into the creek and Agatha's beautiful web was again in ruins.

Audi received the reports with considerable decorum and suggested that the snails perform their construction defenses before the current dry spell rendered them defenseless. Nerva agreed and left as quickly as his physique would allow.

On the fifth sun, the headquarters' staff awoke early to the cicadas' alarm carefully coordinated with the crickets and katydids. They sounded like there were millions of them, and though it portended a life-and-death engagement, the engineered sound encouraged the army. The defenses were quickly rallied. Audi saw what appeared to be tens of thousands of paper wasps holding fire ants as they rose from the ground behind a barrage of mosquitoes. Earwigs, wolf spiders, and centipedes followed at a cautious distance. The plan

worked brilliantly. As soon as the mosquitoes smelled one of the people, they swarmed around the person until thousands of fire ants were dropped to begin a savage stinging attack. Sometimes the people were completely encased in the nest. In these instances, the fire ants were dropped on the nest and, following the lead of the mosquitoes, ultimately penetrated the nest, stinging the inhabitant ceaselessly.

In all such cases, after penetration had been made, it was only a short time before the movable nests hastily withdrew. The mantis's plan was largely successful, and four of the biggest nests resisted all attack efforts. These four seemed to be doubly enraged at the effort made against them. Staying close to the creek where the trees were smaller, they formed a column and began a violent advance toward the thicket and the hollow tree. Everyone knew this would be their last stand.

The cicadas, katydids, and crickets fell back as the enemy advanced but kept up their battle cry with greater vigor than ever. Audi sent wave after wave of spiders to the front in the event any of the people should leave their nests. None did. Still the ground troops carefully waited for their opportunity.

When the huge nests began to close in on the thicket, the headquarters staff prepared to exit the area altogether. As they formed an orderly retreat, the sound of the cicada/cricket chorus reached a noisy climax. Involuntarily Audi and Agatha looked up to witness the arrival of clouds of honeybees. For some reason their appearance reversed the retreating defensive force. The army began a counterattack. The swarms of bees eventually began amassing on the clear portion at the front of each of the nests. Miraculously, as the amassing was completed, each of the nests halted. Then Haydn arrived, smiling broadly in greeting. Without so much as a word, he grabbed Audi, placing him on his thorax, and flew into a tree near the stopped nests. The cicada/cricket chorus was loud, and the air and ground forces were filled with determination. It was a moving sight.

It took various lengths of time, but in every case but one, the people eventually jumped from the nest and ran, followed by swarms of air and ground forces. With each step, members of the ground troops attached themselves to the people, turning the defeat into a rout. Haydn and Audi observed from the tree that the retreating enemy was greatly slowed by the tangle of half-chewed bushes and plants that the snails had so effectively accomplished. Haydn had a feeling that once the people escaped this time, they wouldn't quickly return. And if they did, he definitely knew how to slow and stop them.

CHAPTER 13

• • • • • • • • • • • •

Delivering the Deathblow

Everyone waited around the last nest until evening. Little by little the cicadas and their colleagues quit chirping (they had done an excellent job), and as darkness fell, everything became entirely quiet. Haydn and Audi returned to the ledge in the tree and found it covered with insects and other assorted creatures. Jubilant faces were everywhere in the hollow, made brilliant by the presence of hundreds of fireflies. The crowd seemed to rush toward Haydn at once to congratulate him for his successful battle strategy. Haydn in each case was quick to point out that it was the cooperation of the entire group that had saved their world. The celebration lasted well into the night.

After the rejoicing died down, the merrymakers began falling asleep. In the ensuing silence, Haydn saw Agatha for the first time since the battle had ended. The two warmly embraced; it was a peculiar sight: two predators locked not in battle but affection. She added her thanks for Haydn's success too. Then she reached down and patted sleeping Audi on his red abdomen, commending him to Haydn for his serious handling of matters while Haydn was gone.

"Incidentally," she said, "how did you finally convince the bees to help out?"

"I went back to the same hive we had previously visited and explained the situation. The queen had been impressed with our first visit and agreed not only to send her hive, but also to send messengers out to many other hives as well."

"May I inquire why it took so long for the bees to arrive?" interrupted Agatha.

"In order to get the hive to swarm, the queen actually has to leave the hive and it's a major undertaking. So we had to notify all of the queens that it was time to leave, and then there was the actual flying time. All in all, I think we did pretty well," Haydn said.

"You did do fine; we all did. We accomplished a great task, the achievement of a lifetime. I was wondering…"

Agatha's question had halted so abruptly that Haydn felt a wave of uneasiness pass through his body. Looking over his shoulder, he saw a strong shaft of light, definitely too bright for fireflies; moreover, the light was moving. Then a sound could be heard…breathing. Finally, at the entrance of the hollow tree, very close to where Agatha and Haydn stood talking, one of the people entered, aiming the shaft of light throughout the tree.

Haydn's eyes followed the shaft as it exposed tens

of thousands of the sleeping troops, exhausted from the day's events. As the shaft started moving along the ledge, Haydn slipped behind a piece of wood, trying in vain to get Agatha to move with him, but the spider was too slow and the light exposed her. In the next instant, sensing danger, Haydn raced into the light, his wings completely unfolded. The ruse failed. Haydn saw in the shadow the massive appendage rising, prepared for its crushing descent.

But then, inexplicably, the appendage grabbed the back of the enemy's own neck amid loud sounds. The noise alerted the fireflies whose light steadily increased. The figure in the door was now removing what seemed to be a covering from its head. When the head was exposed, the eyes could plainly be seen; they were open wide with a maniacal look in them, and a steady sound was emanating from the mouth, obviously in some sort of communication. Haydn noticed the enemy holding up a shiny object, which suddenly burst into flame. The noise on the floor bespoke the panic each of the awakening troops felt at the sight of fire. Then a piercing scream filled the air, the flame disappeared, and the enemy crumpled in the doorway. In a moment, all was quiet again.

By this time, the fireflies had totally illumined the tree. Most of the occupants of the tree had not fully awakened, including Audi, who sat quietly, still not comprehending what had occurred.

Haydn and Agatha peered down at the motionless would-be assassin. Agatha broke the silence. "Watch out! The head covering is moving!"

Out from under the folds of the head covering crept a large shadow that, upon contact with the air, flew up to the ledge. It was Phaedra.

"I didn't know you were capable of flight," Agatha said.

"Very capable, in fact," Phaedra replied. "I had been following the enemy since he left his nest after dark. I believe he was going to burn down our headquarters, so I attacked. Obviously I penetrated his defensive covering."

"But why, would someone explain why, he collapsed after removing the head gear?" Agatha asked.

"Hey, some of you fireflies, get nearer the head of the enemy. Get some light down there," commanded Haydn.

Soon hundreds of fireflies hovered near the victim's head, revealing several strands of familiar-looking silk wound around the victim's head and neck. Coming out from the back of the victim's neck was a shiny black spider.

"Adamantine!" Agatha whispered throatily.

Everyone on the floor backed away as the black widow made her dramatic exit. Haydn noticed that Audi watched in undistracted fascination and that the wolf spiders raced to get a look at the Untouchable until she

reached her lifeline, which she used to climb to the top of the hollow "tree" where she disappeared without a word. Agatha didn't fail to spot a large egg sac in the webbing where the spider disappeared.

"So she does care a little," she said to herself.

CHAPTER 14
· · · · · · · · · · · ·
A Permanent
Preserve of Peace

In the light of morning, Haydn began issuing directives. Everyone was told to maintain a strictly defensive posture: no cicada/cricket/katydid warning unless the nests started moving up the creek again. Everyone was to remain out of sight unless the attack resumed. It never did.

In the suns that followed, the nests and the enemy's body were removed by other people with no resistance from the creatures. Each morning saw the arrival of various contingents of the army. Word spread that an enormous cloud of butterflies had been seen near the Path of Great Danger. It was decided that everyone who could should meet at the place where the podium rock once stood to welcome them back.

The morning of their arrival was the happiest morning anyone could remember. Haydn was delighted to see so many that had given so much to the effort. Early on he met the protocol drone (as proper as ever) who, together with Honey, brought greetings from the bees. Later he saw Simmons with his wasp and mud dauber friends buzzing a vapid conversation. Despite the many smaller celebrants, Phaedra and her consort managed to reach Haydn. Phaedra had her hooked, clawlike legs outstretched in a frightening gesture that caused Audi to hop. She didn't seem to notice but warmly greeted everyone and even allowed Audi to inspect her eggs deployed prominently on her husband's back.

Agatha saw and talked to the mother centipede that she had met on the first day of her recruiting effort. They spent quite some time reviewing their perspectives of the war. She also was pleased to see the wolf spider who had saved her life on that fateful morning in the hollow. They both were covered with tears from their many eyes as they recalled the shared moment.

Then, in the midst of the hubbub, Mustabug arrived, carried by a legion of fire ants. He was accompanied by several of his loyal fans, including, to Haydn's surprise, the blind dobsonfly! Mustabug formally introduced Audi and Haydn to Zula, who was being carried by the fire ants along with several of her nectar ant subjects. Mustabug had regained his decorum but looked a little haggard.

Thus everyone was on hand as the first small butterflies heralded their general approach. For the rest of the morning and early afternoon, they came—a billowing, brilliantly colored collection of butterflies dancing and wheeling through the air. It was spectacular! During the height of the gala event, Haydn, Audi, Agatha, and Mustabug stood side by side, smiling radiantly at the crowds and each other. Audi occasionally did his little circle dance to Haydn's amusement. They all savored the moment together.

At one point Haydn leaned over to Mustabug and said, "It was grand, wasn't it?"

"Grand and glorious," the scarab answered. "Grand and glorious!"

As the last of the butterflies appeared, the entire assembly exploded into spontaneous applause. The cicadas, crickets, and katydids chirped wildly as they caught sight of not one or two but hundreds of beautifully colored luna moths sweep into view. Haydn was delighted, and Mustabug burst into tears.

"We did it. We're really safe!" he said.

The rest of his words were drowned out in the din. The ensuing pandemonium lasted through the afternoon and well into the night. It was a celebration no one would ever forget. All too soon though, the festivities were over and the physically and emotionally exhausted crowds began drifting back to the woods— their woods—to the world they had saved.

In time, the fabric of life resumed its normal routine. Even Mustabug eventually returned to the dung pile to take up his duties as a seer. Haydn, Audi, and Agatha remained friends through the summer and into

the late fall. On warm nights, they sometimes stood by the slow-moving creek and watched the fireflies in their nighttime gambols under the stars. And occasionally they recounted that fateful yet strangely wonderful period when the woods were saved by an intellectual praying mantis, a genteel arachnid, and an audacious jumping spider.

The End

CPSIA information can be obtained
at www.ICGtesting.com
Printed in the USA
BVHW09s0711111018
529837BV00028B/1225/P